LADY LILITH

Carm Ianiri

Copyright © 2019 Carm Ianiri
All rights reserved
First Edition

PAGE PUBLISHING, INC.
New York, NY

First originally published by Page Publishing, Inc. 2019

ISBN 978-1-68456-585-6 (Paperback)
ISBN 978-1-68456-587-0 (Hardcover)
ISBN 978-1-68456-586-3 (Digital)

Printed in the United States of America

CHAPTER ONE

Peering at the sapphire sky, Lilianna could only hear the calmness of the seawater as she lay in her father's abandoned fishing boat. Her *sanctuary,* in the port of her beloved hometown of Portici, had been sitting idle for a year since his death. Luckily, it remained one of a handful of vessels that had not been completely destroyed by the vicious bombings of the ports. Lili would escape the oppression of reality and war by taking refuge on the cherished little ark.

It was July 1945, and Portici had just been relieved by American Allied forces as the hostilities of World War II had finally come to an end a couple of months earlier. The town, situated at the foot of the volcano Mount Vesuvius, sat on the Bay of Naples. Portici was also coping with the remnants of the last eruption, which had taken place in March 1944. Naples was the most bombed Italian city in World War II, particularly due to its port facilities, which were the primary targets. The economy had collapsed, and the city, along with its surrounding areas, was in ruins. The Allies were stationed throughout the cities and towns to prevent starvation and keep order.

"Liliana!" a voice from the distance called out. Lili peeked over the edge to see her sister, Rosanna, standing on the dock of the port.

"Yes, I'm here," hollered Lilly.

"Come home now. Mamma is waiting," Rose shouted angrily. Lili realized she had fallen asleep when she closed her eyes to recall the many fond memories of her now-deceased father.

Paolo Bianchi was an avid fisherman who provided for his family by employing himself with an occupation he loved. As a child, Lili would accompany him every day.

"Liliana," muttered Dahlia as Lilly entered the home, "where have you been all this time?"

"I'm sorry, Mamma," Lili apologized.

"She's always in that silly boat," snarled Rose.

Rosanna, who was nine years her senior, was the older sister Lili idolized. Although Rose did not meet the popular standards of beauty, her confidence and poise were very alluring. She also possessed other distinctions like sexual attractiveness that were appealing especially to men. Rose stood tall and slim, with shoulder-length dark-brown curls and brown eyes. Her main focus in life was seeking attention, particularly from the males. Despite Lili's admiration for her, Rose's perception of her little sister was anything but of admiration.

Unlike Rose, who was bold and engaging, Lili was demure and timid. Yet Lili was the sister who acquired all the bodily and intellectual beauty. She was petite however buxom and voluptuous. At the age of sixteen, she was already displaying a maturity beyond her years, both physically and mentally.

With her amazing long auburn locks parted to one side and hazel-green eyes, Lili was captivating and beloved. But her insecurities and modesty kept her from dreams and achievements. Lili would always remain the destitute town girl unlike her older sister. Rose's determination and tenacity would one day get her out of Portici and even possibly Italy.

"Mamma, I'm going to my room. I'm really tired," Lili said quietly as she arose from the dining chair.

"Oh dio mio, do you do nothing but sleep or lie around all day and night? If you're not hiding in that silly boat, you're hiding in your room! You will never go anywhere in life if you keep doing that. You won't even find a husband!" pestered Rose.

"Rosanna, enough," snapped Dahlia at her audacious older daughter. "I am very tired of all this foolishness. You must stop this at once!"

Rose had a troubling envy toward her baby sister. She never called her Lili or Liliana. She would always refer to her as *Lilith*. *Lilith* was a mythological figure who was envisioned as a dangerous demon of the night. However, *Lilith* was also considered a sex goddess. Rose always joked that Paolo and Dahlia named her baby sister appropriately. She didn't believe Lili was as angelic as everyone made her out to be. Rose might have been the wicked one between the two, but she felt there was a hidden side to Lili she masked very well.

"Your inamorato has arrived," Dahlia amusingly added.

"Ciao, amore mio," Rose shouted as she strolled to open the door.

Luca Marchese was a local carpenter who had been Rose's love interest for the past two years. He was slender, with dark hair and deep crystal-like eyes that would make many young girls and women swoon. His body was chiseled and fit, like that of a Michelangelo statue.

Rose was already twenty-four years old, and most women were usually married by the age of twenty-one. She was considered an "old maid" already by the traditionalists. Luca was looking forward to a comfortable and serene future with Rose one day. However, despite Luca's deep affection for her, Rose was uncertain he was the one destined for her. She always had high expectations for herself, and that included whomever she would choose as a future partner.

Rose's confidence and determination would never allow her to settle for anything less than what she felt she deserved.

"My life cannot be in Portici forever," Rose often grumbled to herself. Her ultimate dream was to go to the United States. But how? Plus she had a devoted, handsome lover who wanted nothing more than to marry *her*. Luca was a wonderful man. Yet a severe obstacle stood in their way that intensely disturbed Rose. Luca was born with a notable absence of gonads. He possessed a disorder that caused missing testicles.

Sex with Luca was sweet, and he always tried desperately to demonstrate his ability to pleasure a woman. However, it was rare that Rose would reach orgasm, and his condition was of enormous concern to her. His libido was not as active as most men, so it was difficult for him to have an erection. Rose's sexual desires were much higher, and she craved a partner whose intensity matched hers.

As much as Luca wanted to marry Rosanna, she knew deep down inside she would probably not marry him. Rose would find her haven at the Orto Botanico di Portici, where there were plenty of the soldiers. Just like her little sister, Lili, who would seek refuge on her father's boat, Rose found pleasure in the botanical gardens. They were being used as a military-vehicle compound by the Allied forces during the war.

In 1935, the Royal Palace of Portici, situated on the grounds of the gardens, was a school that had become a part of the University of Naples. It was transformed into the botanical gardens by the school's first botany professor, Nicola Antonio Pedicino. The sprawling grounds offered diverse landscapes, from wetlands to rose gardens. Unfortunately, many plants had been destroyed from the occupation of the Allied troops.

The palace in the gardens had once been the home of Charles III of Spain before it became the Royal Higher School of Agriculture. Rose would frequent the grounds to stare at the majestic facade of the palace and watch the soldiers of the university strolling or studying. With its avenue of trees and battered statues, one could also catch views of Vesuvius and the sea.

Even after surviving the ravages of World War II, the palace grounds remained a place where art, nature, and science all collided. It had become the place for Rose to find peace and asylum, although mostly to gaze at the many handsome Allied soldiers.

"Buon giorno, signorina," called out a distinguished masculine voice.

As Rose turned, she saw three American soldiers.

"She looks like a nice piece of ass." One of the others cackled.

Then a different voice deflected, "Have some respect."

"Oh, relax, Manny. She doesn't understand."

Rose looked at all of them sternly, with her arms crossed defensively, and scolded, "Oh really?"

Rose spoke and understood the English language well by self-teaching with books and radio.

"Thank you, sir. You are very kind," she acknowledged the dashing soldier for defending her honor.

"You are very welcome," he responded in the manliest and sexiest voice she had ever heard.

Rose couldn't stop herself from staring at this admirable gentleman. She had seen hundreds of soldiers every day, but this man in particular stood out from the rest. He was tall, muscular, and one of the most handsome men she had ever seen. What made him more exceptional was that he was an American.

Standing by the statue of Flora facing the Palazzo Reale, Rose found herself mesmerized by the charm and intrigue of this stranger.

Oh dio! she thought to herself. Her dream of meeting an American had come true. The odds of encountering him on the royal palace grounds made her all the more believe this was fate.

Rose would have to manage a way to lure herself into this man's heart and mind. She knew, however, that her confidence and determination would guarantee this liaison. This man could possibly take her to America, as many soldiers had previously done or were planning to do. The Italian American GIs especially wanted the Italian girls even if most of the soldiers didn't.

About one million Italian Americans fought in the war and were the largest ethnic group in the military. Consequently, there were plenty of them, much to the delight of the local women.

Naples and its surrounding towns had become the largest resting ground for the Allies.

The city was governed by corruption and the mafia known as the Camorra. As the city grew hopeless, a thriving black market emerged within the city's broken walls. People became desperate, and so crime and prostitution started flourishing.

"Would you like to take a walk with me?" the handsome soldier whispered in Rose's ear.

Shocked yet delighted at his request, she quickly replied, "Yes!" He softly guided her by the arm away from the statue where his fellow soldiers were situated.

"Easy, Manny." One of them snickered. "The ladies here are money-mad and snakes." He quickly forgot Rose could understand him. After peering at him with an angry glare, she turned to her handsome soldier.

"Thank you again. I am Rosanna, and who might you be?" Rose conveyed seductively. She made sure to stare into his deep, sparkling eyes and then at his moist, full lips as to signal her desire to kiss him.

As they wandered the footpaths bounded by dense foliage, Rose would learn that Manuele Catalano was of Italian descent, born in Brooklyn, New York. He had been deployed to Naples for Operation Avalanche, where he served under General Sir Harold Alexander's Fifteenth Army group.

"I must go now, but please, can I see you again tomorrow?" Manny sheepishly asked.

"Yes, of course!" Rose shouted a little more loudly and excitedly than she wanted to sound.

"Okay, tomorrow at 2:00 p.m., I will be waiting for you at the statue where we met today," he said, winking at her.

Rose tried to remain calm and collected and simply replied, "See you then."

As he turned to walk away, she became startled at his quick exit of the gardens. Disappointed, she wondered why he hadn't even given her a kiss on the cheek. Then she realized although he was of Italian descent, he was an American, and they were not accustomed to the same common practices of the Italians.

I have finally found him, Rose rejoiced while crunching through the city's broken glass and rubble. The streets were still littered and polluted from the remnants of war. Yet the tiny apartment along Corso Umberto, which she shared with her mother and sister, was situated in the best part of town. It was right between the Porto del

Granatello, where her father's boat was docked, and the Botanical Gardens, where the Royal Palace was located. It was convenient for both Lili, who sought refuge in her father's fishing boat, and her, who sought refuge at the gardens.

Despite all the chaos and confusion the war had brought, it was finally over. Their mother, Dahlia, unfortunately would find refuge only in their home and barely ever left the apartment. For the past year, she had gone through grief since the death of her husband. Yet she was not feeling well also. While her daughters were mostly outdoors, Dahlia worked as a seamstress to make extra money. This made it easier for her not to have to leave her home. Some women, but mostly men, would come to her apartment for the usual alterations, hems, tear fixes, zipper mending, and other sewing services.

Dahlia's body was swollen and aching. Always feeling pain in her muscles, she had recently been spending more time in her bed than on her sewing machine. Although she was tired, weak, and disheartened, she had two daughters she needed to take care of—especially Lili.

Lili was the delicate and fragile one of the two. Dahlia knew she needed not worry about Rose. She had turned into a bold and fearless young woman who could take care of herself.

But Lili, poor Lili, she thought to herself, *still young and feeble.* The thought of Lili's vulnerability brought tears to Dahlia's eyes and more pain to her heart.

Dahlia loved both her daughters, but Lilianna was special for some reason. Several years after Rose was born, Lili arrived. Dahlia instantly recognized she was an angelic and virtuous soul, traits that would infuriate Rose for years to come. Dahlia was disturbed her older daughter, Rosanna, had grown a resentment and annoyance for Liliana. She was further angered when Rose began calling her *Lilith* instead of Lili.

Even though Mussolini had been overthrown and the war was over, the situation in Italy had actually gotten worse. As consequences of the war lingered, Dahlia was struggling to survive and to feed her daughters. She had to endure all the agony and burden for the past year without her husband. This resulted in her disheveled appearance and being jaded. Her daughter Lili had inherited the same stature as her mother. Dahlia was petite yet curvaceous and ample. At the age of forty-three years, she could still catch the eyes of many men.

What had caused Rosanna to have such malice toward her baby sister? Was it because Lili was gifted with both beauty and brilliance? Still, Lili's innocence and humility would never waver Rose's contempt. Nevertheless, even she was cognizant of Rose's envy of her despite how young and naive Lili was.

Why such malice? Lili pondered this concept as she lay in her father's boat. As she began to close her eyes, a voice shouted out to her; only this time it wasn't Rose.

"Liliana! Are you in there?" asked someone in a masculine tone.

"Luca?" answered Lili. She seemed puzzled and confused as to why he, of all people, would be searching for her. As he ran toward the boat, he said more quietly, "Can I sit with you for a few moments?"

"Ahh, okay, I guess," Lili hesitantly replied. Still perplexed by his request, she quickly pointed out, "But only for a few moments. You are my sister's *ragazzo*, and no one should see us together."

As Luca sat down in front of Lili, he could not help but stare at her. How did he not notice this beautiful, angelic face before? This young girl sitting in front of him was delicate and lovely. As Lili looked at him, mystified, he began asking her, "Where has Rose been? It's been a few days now, and I don't hear from her. The last time I saw her, she said she was helping your sick mother," Luca stated quite sternly.

Lili understood his frustration, and judging from his tone, he did not believe Rose's excuse. Lili knew her sister had been lying to him. Rose wasn't assisting her ailing mother. She was too preoccupied with the American soldier she encountered every day.

Completely smitten and infatuated, Rose spent all her energy making sure this man would be her husband one day. Even the sex was incredible.

"What a difference between Manuele and Luca when it comes to making love," she swooned.

Manny was strong and aggressive, just the way Rose liked it. She had met not only a husband prospect but also someone as animalistic as she was when it came to sexuality. During another encounter, one day, Manny escorted Rose to a building that had been bombed and abandoned. It was there he seduced this engaging woman. She wasn't the most beautiful woman he had ever seen, but there was something about her presence. He appreciated her desire and lust and saw them in her captivating eyes.

Among the erupted Mount Vesuvius soot and war-torn ruins, Rose and Manny began kissing and exploring each other's mouths with their tongues. She felt his hands remove her tucked blouse from her skirt when her whole body trembled with elation.

Moving his hands up from her waist to her breasts, Manny whispered in her ear, "I want you." As he began to fondle and finger her nipples, she realized that there was no turning back. Manny was seducing her, and she was more than excited to participate in this game of persuasion. Rose knew exactly where it was going to end.

After removing her blouse from over her head, his lips and tongue started working their way down from her lips to her neck, slowing down to her breasts. Rose's body felt numb yet tingled at the same time. As Manny placed her gently down onto a block of cold concrete, she quickly found herself spreading her legs as far as her skirt would allow. He, too, had unzipped his trousers so quickly, she thought he was about to ejaculate right there and then. However, despite his gentleness during foreplay, he entered her more forcefully than she had anticipated.

The level of elation and pleasure was far more than anything she had ever experienced before. This was not just intercourse; it felt like primal sex. Although it wasn't dirty or vulgar, it felt uninhibited and assertive. The way he held her and penetrated her forcefully was exciting and exhilarating.

When Manny came inside her, Rose feared it was over. She had not even reached orgasm. However, much to her surprise, he lifted her up and turned her around. With her back to him, he continued to kiss her neck and shoulders then reached around her waist. While one hand caressed and fondled her breast, the other hand started massaging her wet vagina.

Rose whimpered in ecstasy when Manny brought her to orgasm. She could feel her body quivering as she reached her climax. After composing themselves, Manny realized he had probably been away from his base longer than he was allowed. As he took Rose's hand, they started walking hastily back to the gardens. She could feel him pulling at her arm but also understood why he was in such a hurry to return.

Their ten-minute walk back to gardens seemed more like an hour. Not one word was muttered amid its duration. When they finally arrived, Rose was considering how to escape gracefully with her dignity intact. She feared that after Manny got what he wanted, she would never see him again.

Oh dio! she thought to herself. *Could this be the last time we see each other?* What did he think of her? During the war, most women, including ordinary housewives, had become desperate and helpless, so they turned to prostitution.

Military policies attempted to prohibit relationships, both sexual and platonic, causing Rose dread and anxiety after what had just transpired between them.

Would he ever marry such a girl? she feared. Most GIs had judged the Italian women, and Italians in general, as desperate, poor, ignorant, and immoral.

When she began to panic and doubt why she surrendered to him so instantly, Manny leaned over to kiss her on the cheek and quietly whispered, "I'll see you tomorrow, Rosie. Same time, same place." She loved her new nickname, Rosie. It felt so personal and special. She was able to now breathe a bit of a sigh of relief. He had confirmed that they would see each other once again. Rose had no doubt in her mind Manny was just as smitten with her as she was with him. But just as her thoughts were reaching pure frenzy, another thought entered her mind. This quickly disrupted her elation.

"Luca," she mumbled to herself, annoyed.

"What can I do, Luca?" Lili requested quietly with her head down.

"I don't know," whined Luca. "I'm just tired of being her puppet. She is not my puppet master. I will not allow anyone to disrespect me like this!" In an angry tone, Luca continued, "Word around the town is that she has been keeping company with American soldiers. Does she really think they will take her seriously? When they go back to the United States, Naples will only be a distant memory for them!" he shouted angrily.

After two hours of sitting together and listening to this gentleman, Lili found herself confiding in him, too, about her feelings. She felt touched by his display of emotion as she noticed tears streaming down his admirable face.

Wow, he is handsome and so kind, she thought to herself. How could Rose betray someone like this? Lili quickly realized sensitivity was the major distinction between her and her sister.

Rose had always been selfish and couldn't accept her own sister, let alone anyone else. Perhaps Dahlia was the only one Rose did love unconditionally, but even that was questionable. Her attitude toward Lili and lack of empathy for their ailing mother were evidences of Rose's insensitivity. Rose did not have the same connection with their father as Lili did. She would fondly remember her special relationship with him. As a little girl, Lili would accompany her Papa every day to watch him fish. Quite often, Dahlia would accompany them, and all three would spend hours together by the water before the ports of Naples were bombed.

The beginning of World War II had started on September of 1939. However, Naples was not struck until November 1, 1940. Yet Paolo's love for the waters did not deter him until the largest raid, which occurred on August 4, 1943. This was the day he was killed. Still, even after such heavy bombings, his little fishing boat, docked in the port, would somehow remain intact.

One element was definitely evident during these troubled yet cherished times. For Lili it was the absence of her older sister. As far as she could remember, Rose had always been the black sheep of the family. She never wanted to participate in anything that didn't involve boys or romance. According to Lili, Rose lived in a fantasy world. Even during the war, Rose seemed to be in denial. She would only occasionally comment on how handsome some of the soldiers were, especially the Americans. Lili, however, felt quite differently about the Americans; she detested these men.

Heavy raids by the Americans had begun in December 1942, which lasted until the ceasefire with Italy in September 1943. They were massive, and the smell of death still hung in the air, with many dead bodies still rotting under mounds of rubble in the streets.

It was *because of them* that Lili no longer had her Papa. It was *because of them* that her beautiful, picturesque, and once-tranquil hometown was now ravaged with rubble and collapsed buildings. It was *because of them* that her mother was falling ill, with all the diseases that they had brought over. Now, it was *because of them* that her sister had rejected this gentle, lost soul.

Luca realized his relationship with Rose was over. After his conversation with Lili, Luca concluded his future with Rose was not to be. Yet why did he have to fall in love with such a crass and selfish woman?

Observing Lili and speaking with her, Luca couldn't help but wonder how they could possibly be of the same blood. Lili was pure and innocent, courteous and compassionate, and undeniably beautiful.

Oh dio, he reminded himself, *she is so young*. Still, Lili had all the qualities her sister didn't. Rosanna was a woman. Lilianna was still a child.

Rose was an attractive, provocative, and sensual woman whom Luca loved very much and had wanted to build a future with. However, that would never happen. She was ashamed he was only a carpenter and did not serve in the military. Furthermore, she had finally met an American GI.

There was only one man in Rose's eyes, Manuele Catalano. As the days passed, Luca became nothing more than a memory.

However, the task of persuading Manny to ask for her hand in marriage would not be easy.

There had been thousands of marriages between Italian girls and American soldiers, especially with Italian American soldiers. So why couldn't she be one of these war brides? Rose wanted nothing more than to leave Italy, especially Naples. Yet the bias of the US military played a big role in limiting many marriages between American soldiers and Italian women. Rose was familiar with the military easily dismissing many soldiers' marital requests.

Unfortunately, prospective Neapolitan war brides frequently turned out to be notorious prostitutes attempting to find their way into the United States. It undeniably cast doubt on other Italian women and American GIs attempting to marry.

Neapolitan women had acquired quite the reputation when it came to sex. Prostitution had become rampant, so many of the soldiers, out of fear of catching a sexually transmitted disease, wouldn't engage in sexual relations with the women in that area.

Rose wanted so much for her mother to meet this amazing American. It wasn't so much about needing Dahlia's approval but more about boasting to all those around her, starting with her mother. She decided she would ask Manny, when they met again at the gardens, to meet her family.

As Rose entered her mother's bedroom, she firmly announced, "Mamma, I am inviting my fiancé over for dinner tonight!"

As Dahlia lay tired and drained on her bed, she marveled, "Everything is okay now with Luca?"

"Luca?" Rose's tone quickly changed from excited to irritated. "My fiancé is American, and I want both of you to meet him." She glanced over to Lili, who was sitting on the edge of her mother's bed.

"Fiancé?" questioned Lili then continued, "So Luca was right. You have been keeping company with American GIs."

"Only one and I'm going to marry him!" snarled Rose.

"Has he asked you to marry?" sputtered Lili.

"Yes, well, he will. And I will go to the USA with him!" ranted Rose.

"But I am not feeling well, Rosa *mia*. You know this." Dahlia sighed.

"Lilith can cook the dinner and do everything. After all, she is the gifted one," Rose sarcastically bickered. She constantly expressed her jealousy and envy toward her younger sister with disparaging comments.

"Lilith!" Lili shrilled at the nickname Rose had given her. Lilith was known as an ancient demoness. This demoness was the personification of female sexuality with power over men and an enlightener of women. However, Rose's interpretation of Lilith was associated with the female demon known for wind and terror, and she was thought to be a bearer of disease, illness, and death.

How dare Rose call her Lilith, a demoness? She shrieked. Never had she known a sibling so cruel. When Lili looked back at all the horrendous words and acts Rose said and did to her, she would sob in disbelief. Rose was always despicable and defiant while Lili felt defeated.

Over the years, Rose managed to crush and overpower Lili. One of the cruelest acts Rose ever committed was cutting off all Lili's beautiful auburn locks. Lili was only nine years old and traumatized. She couldn't comprehend how her eighteen-year-old sister could be so harsh.

How could a young woman, considered to be an adult, sabotage a little girl due to jealousy and envy? Lili realized at that young age, Rose was an eccentric and irrational human being. Lili tried to love her and form a sisterly bond but would never prevail. Yet for some odd reason, Lili admired Rose. Although her sister was deranged and bizarre, Rose was still her sister.

Lilith wondered if perhaps one day she could live up to her disparaging "nickname." Still, she couldn't imagine being that senseless and irresponsible. Lili could never cause another human being, especially a loved one; such torment and suffering. She had seen enough in the past few years, particularly during the war. This was the most dreadful and atrocious existence anyone could inhabit. If Lili had been more like the mythological *Lilith*, Rose would never get away with violating her sister, Lili often theorized.

CHAPTER TWO

As fearless and as self-assuring as Rose exhibited herself externally, her bitterness toward Lili was at the root of her insecurities and rage. Rose's eagerness to escape Italy was based not only on the devastation created by the war but mostly on the devastation of her self-esteem caused by *Lilith*, devised by her parents and the people around her. They continuously focused their attention on the beautiful, delicate younger flower Lili.

When their father, Paolo, was alive, many of the townsfolk would tease him about his beautiful bouquet—Dahlia, Rose, and Lili. However, it was the youngest blossom of the bunch who seemed to shine and bloom greatest. Rose's personality was the brunt of many jabs, being referred to as the flower with many thorns. Although she would maintain her composure and laugh them off, her resentment would intensify over the years. As more and more people took notice of her little sister's rapid growth into a sensual but virtuous young woman, the more Rose's envy and rage would be enhanced.

After a night of unrest, Rose couldn't wait to see Manny again. They would routinely meet in the gardens, by the statue of Flora as usual. After a good walk and some small talk, they would go to the same place to have their usual, exciting sexual rendezvous.

One afternoon, while Manny was zipping up his trousers, he glanced over at Rose while she was buttoning her blouse. After another session of exciting sex, he turned to her and affirmed, "I'm leaving soon, Rosie."

"What?" Rose shrieked.

"I'm going home to America."

As Rose's eyes began to fill with tears, she abruptly shouted, "Let's get married!" Looking stunned and confused, Manny stared at Rose as she continued, "I don't see why we cannot get married. You mentioned your parents would like you to settle down once you go back to New York."

Contemplating Rose's suggestion, Manny hesitated but then assured, "Sure, why not?"

Rose jumped to wrap her arms around his broad and muscular shoulders. She began kissing him like a mother kissing her child, steadily on his cheeks. She was in a state of euphoria.

Rose's dream of marrying an American had finally materialized. She couldn't wait to run home to confirm her proposal to her ever-doubting mother and baby sister. The following evening, Manny would come over to meet her family, and finally she would be able to gloat. How exciting it was going to be for the imminent marriage to her American GI.

This was truly *most* of her dreams coming true. However, it wasn't exactly the ideal marriage proposal. She would have loved for her future husband to get on one knee, holding and offering a beautiful ring while asking her the big question.

I guess not everything can be perfect, she pondered, hoping this was not a bad sign. As long as it would take her away from the wartorn landscape and situation of Naples, it didn't matter.

"The least you can do is brush that disheveled mane of yours!" asserted Rose as she rolled her eyes and walked by. Lili, looking confused, turned to look into the mirror hanging on the wall, over the tiny dining table.

"Oh dio!" Lili gasped. Her usual olive-colored skin was looking ghastly white, and her hair looked like it had not been managed for days. She could not present herself to her future brother-in-law in this grim manner.

"*Lilith*, how are things coming along?" Rose chuckled sarcastically. As Lili was scrambling to clean up the mess she had made from preparing dinner, she wondered what possessed her to agree to make this special feast. Why all this fuss for an older sister who clearly did not appreciate her and whose animosity was always evident? Then Lili reminded herself, *This isn't for Rose. This is for Mamma.*

To watch her mother quickly deteriorate over the past few weeks was getting very troublesome. Lili was still haunted by the death of her father. The thought of losing her mother was unthinkable. To imagine life without them was already unbearable, and to be left alone with only her insensitive, selfish sister brought Lili much anxiety and dread.

"Mamma, Manny will be here soon. Can you please try to get yourself up from that bed?" Rose pleaded with her mother.

"I will try my best. Let me just wash my face and change into fresh clothes." Dahlia sighed. Rose's attire was a swing-style dress, with wide padded shoulders, nipped high at the waist, and A-line skirt that came down to the knee. Her hair was perfectly coiffed, and her lips were purposely stained ruby red to give herself a sexier look. She didn't possess the ideal curvy hourglass shape like Lili, but she always tried to make the most of her slim and lanky figure.

After hearing a couple of knocks at the door, Rose quickly rushed to inform her mother and sister to come out of their rooms. As she opened the door and saw her handsome GI standing in the doorway, she couldn't help but throw her arms around him. Rose had not felt this happy and excited in years.

As she took off his overcoat, Dahlia appeared at the hallway entrance.

"You must be Mrs. Bianchi. I'm Manny. It is a pleasure to finally meet you. Now I know where Rose gets her good looks," he affirmed. Dahlia was flushed while shaking his hand. Manny could see that Dahlia was frail and weak. He quickly reached for her arm to place her down in the chair.

"Grazie, and please sit down, both of you. Lilianna will be out in a few moments." As the three of them were getting acquainted for the next few minutes, Rose's impatience was becoming evident.

"Lilith! We are hungry. Hurry, please!" Rose shouted, clinching her teeth. The look on Manny's face turned from bliss to bafflement. He couldn't believe she would speak to someone in this manner. While staring at her, dazed, he thought to himself, *She's like a snobby aristocrat commanding a servant.*

As Rose looked over to Manny, she noticed his change of expression from bewilderment to astonishment. When she turned her head to observe where Manny was staring, Lili had emerged.

"It's about time!" Rose scolded harshly.

As Lili approached the dining table, Rose watched in fright as Manny couldn't keep his eyes off her. Lili was the most beautiful girl he had ever seen. For a few moments, it seemed his world had stopped. Everything around him blurred into oblivion and disappeared. Everything had dissolved except her beautiful face. As their eyes met, Lili became puzzled by the sudden attraction she felt for this man. He was an American man that was considered an enemy not long ago. A part of her was captivated, yet another was enraged.

This man was one of the individuals responsible for the destruction of her country. The destruction resulted in starvation, dehumanization, and the death of thousands around her. Most of all, he was responsible for the demise of her beloved father. He was a murderer. These American invaders had taken so many lives.

Rose watched in exasperation and despair while observing the look on Manny's face. He stood up and introduced himself.

"Hello. You must be Lili. I'm Manny."

"Yes, I know who you are," Lili uttered. Quickly realizing how rudely she sounded, she promptly continued, "Please sit down," gesturing with her hand. "Dinner is ready."

"Grazie," replied Manny, still fixated on her face and unable to take his eyes off her.

What were these unexplainable sentiments he was feeling? Manny had met so many women throughout his life in America and abroad. And he had no problem igniting any woman's fire as most of them fancied him also. Yet this innocent young girl was so beautiful and divine, he felt like he lost all his senses. His stomach jolted, and he felt dizzy and numb. Although he was aware of how young she was, he felt deliriously happy. All these frightful emotions flowing through him were a perfect fusion of ecstasy and fear.

"Please forgive me, Manny. I am not very well. So if you will excuse me, I will go to my room for some rest," Dahlia apologized.

"It was a pleasure to finally meet you and your beautiful daughter."

Beautiful daughter? Rose's reaction went from being flustered to outrage after hearing this. She shrilled, "Manny and I will be in the parlor while you clean this mess!"

No one had touched the food. However, the truth was, none of them could eat. Dahlia was too weak to put anything in her mouth. Manny was too enraptured by Lili, and Rose was too infuriated.

I'm so sick of everyone loving Lilith! she seethed.

As Lili sat alone at the kitchen table, she began to evaluate the situation. She picked at some of her food and wondered what had just happened. Her mother was deteriorating at a rapid pace; her sister's defiance was becoming more and more evident. But who was this mysterious man whom she loathed yet was so intrigued by?

Although enticed by him, Lili but quickly reminded herself that this soldier was soon to be her brother-in-law. After an hour of listening to him tell his stories of his home life in America and his experience abroad, Lili was perplexed. How could a man with his ethics want to marry a woman like Rose? She was anything but ethical and much more deceitful and selfish than most women.

Growing up, Lili had always admired her older sister; however, her admiration had deflated enormously as the days passed. She had discovered the extreme of Rose's greed and narcissism, especially now that she was anticipating marriage to an American GI. While Rose prepared her papers and was busy planning her wedding, Lili was confined to her home. She was dedicated to taking care of their ailing mother, who was rapidly withering away.

Dahlia had become so weak and frail. She was experiencing excruciating pain. When both she and Lili heard the door close, they realized Manny had left.

"Rosanna," she called out. Lili was already sitting at the end of her bed. "Please come to me," Dahlia summoned. As soon as Rose walked into the room, she continued, "I need both of you to sit beside me and listen." As tears started rolling down Dahlia's face, both Rose and Lili looked at each other with confusion. "I don't know how much longer I can hold on."

Lili cried out, "Mamma! Stop, please!"

"My beautiful *flowers*." Dahlia paused. "I am very sick, and you see this." As Lili burst into tears, she laid her head down on her mother's chest.

Rose huffed, "But you can't miss my wedding!" For the first time, Lili glared at her sister that it even startled Rose.

Typical selfish Rose, Lili thought to herself.

"I will not miss your wedding, my lovely Rosa," Dahlia reassured her.

"I must tell Manny it's necessary that we marry quickly!" Rose blurted. Lili stared at her sister in wonder and disbelief; she was more concerned about her wedding than her dying mother. Lili then walked toward her mother's closet to get Dahlia's wedding dress. After taking it out, Lili suggested, "You should wear Mamma's dress for your wedding."

"It is so old! I can't wear that!" snarled Rose.

Lili knew that Rose had no intention of wearing the gown. She just wanted to look and feel the dress again. Maybe one day she could wear it. As she walked past her mother; Lili couldn't help but notice how jaundiced Dahlia looked. It was at that moment Lili realized her mother was very close to death.

As the tears flowed down her cheeks, Lili knelt down before the bed. She then placed her arms on the warm but worn out blanket covering her mother's fragile body and began to pray. Rose had walked back to her own room.

Lili's faith was always much deeper than that of her parents and even more so than that of Rose. She would frequent the Rettoria Dell'Immacolata a Cappella Reale, located close to her home. She would attend regular mass and often go to confession. From the day her father passed away, she would stop in every day to say a prayer. Lately she said several prayers in the hope that her mother would get well again. The church was the only place these days she would go, when not at home taking care of her mother.

Rose, on the other hand, was way too busy to stay at home. She spent all her days frolicking the streets. She made sure all the town's women were informed of her fortune. She was going to become an American bride and was soon embarking on a new journey.

Rose reveled in the attention immensely. Not only was she chosen by such a handsome American GI to be his bride, but she could finally go to the United States. She was permanently leaving behind the tragic life of Portici and of Italy.

Manny frequently wrote his parents and had informed them of his intended marriage. Yet he found himself questioning his decision to marry Rose.

What did I do? He was very fond of her but wasn't in love with her. He wasn't even sure if his parents would like her.

How could he think about marriage to Rose? All he could think of was Lili. Since the moment he laid his eyes on her, he knew he had come face-to-face with new emotions he had never sensed before. He was lovestruck. But was this just an infatuation or impulsiveness and delusions? Manny worried.

Still, this wasn't just about her beauty and innocence. She was sincere and humble, something his future wife was not. What had struck him more so was her devotion and compassion for her mother. Unlike Rose, Lili was completely dedicated to taking care of Dahlia. To him, these were signs of selflessness, kindness, and pure love.

Thereafter, Manny would quite often stop in to see how Dahlia was doing. This also allowed him to see Lili. When she looked at him, he would feel his body freeze and could not look away. His heart would beat rapidly; his mind would race, and he felt indescribable breathlessness.

Every time Manny laid his eyes on Lili, everything else around him would cease. He knew he was encompassing an enrapturing sensation that was a genuine feeling. He was also conscious of Lili's reluctance of him. She made it obvious. Nevertheless, he recognized there was a strong connection between them and could see the desire in her eyes.

Lili's contempt for him was strictly a stance she was taking in her mind. She considered him the enemy. Yet in her heart were unexplainable feelings.

How could this be? she speculated every time she was in his presence.

Lili detested these contrasting emotions for Manny. Her heart and mind were constantly battling each other. She was raised with integrity, but he made her feel so helpless and immoral.

Manny was also battling his own despair. He was very doubtful of his up-and-coming wedding.

The civil service had already been arranged, so the next plan was some sort of reception. Although the war was over, there weren't any places available for a peacetime affair. With no money forthcoming, a reception venue was out of the question. Most wartime weddings and functions were celebrations held at home. How could Rose and Manny have a reception at her mother's tiny apartment? Rose fretted. She realized her anticipation of going to America far outweighed her desire for an elaborate wedding. Instead, she would ask Manny's parents to throw them a fancy party when they arrived.

Rose had learned that Manny's family was affluent in the garment industry. After much research on her part, Rose discovered they owned a lucrative clothing factory. They had plenty of money. The past five years had been especially profitable since the invasion of France in May 1940. In Paris, the fashion industry laid siege for this duration, and many of its fashion houses had closed. With the French firmly smothered, the American fashion industry took over.

The wedding day had finally arrived, and while Rose was ecstatic, Lili was furious. How could her sister not consider wearing her mother's bridal dress? Dahlia had created and sewn it herself. To Lili, it was an heirloom, a beautiful creation from Dahlia's talents. Yet according to Rose, it was far too old and outdated.

All the adornments of prewar fashion dressing were now thought of as very bad taste, and the simplification of style had become essential. So Rose opted for an exceptionally fashionable beige and fine wool crepe French dress. It had a matching jacket and pillbox hat with a net veil in front to cover the eyes. Her hair was swept to one side and flat to accommodate her hat while the other side had voluminous curls, known as the victory roll, that framed her face.

Manny looked exceptionally handsome in his US Army officer service uniform. He had never been so nervous or hesitant about anything in his life. Even combat hadn't frightened him as much as this day. He knew deep down he wasn't in love with Rose. When Rose walked up with Lili and Dahlia in tow, Manny stared only at Lili.

Lili wore a powder-blue A-line dress that came down to the knee. Her natural hourglass figure—with big breasts, broad shoulders, tiny waist, and full hips—was more than Manny could handle. As he watched the women approach him, he couldn't help but get an erection.

Oh my god, he feared. Manny dreaded the thought of anyone noticing, especially Lili. Dahlia was too weak and frail to notice anything. As she walked arm and arm with Lili, slowly, she could feel herself worsening. However, much to her relief, the ceremony was quick and over in no time.

Both Dahlia and Lili were pleased Rose and Manny had not planned a wedding reception. The marriage was a brief civil service performed by a government official of Portici. Once it was over, Lili and Dahlia headed back to their apartment, and his military friends reported back to their command post. Rose and Manny were invited back to his base for a luncheon prepared by some of his fellow service men.

Although they were married now, Manny would remain at his base until he could be sent back home. Meanwhile Rose was set to depart in a week along with many other Italian war brides. She found it distressing and unusual that she would get to the US before her husband. Generally, GIs were transported home with their brides. Manny insisted he had to stay behind at the request of his commander. He reassured her that his family would take care of her once she reached New York.

As the week passed, Rose was becoming more and more disturbed at the notion of her husband not being with her. She was even more annoyed that the only time they had sex since they were married was their wedding night. Manny wasn't his usual self even that night. Neither one of them had climaxed during sex. Rose could feel he had something on his mind.

Lili was spending all her days taking care of her incapacitated mother. She realized it was only a matter of time before Dahlia would succumb to her illness. Her mother was dying, yet she had no idea what had caused her mother to become so severely ill. Lili was aware of the all the diseases and epidemics the war had brought on. But no one, including Dahlia, would tell Lili what illness she was suffering from.

The day had finally arrived for Rose to embark on the USAHS *Algonquin* leaving from Naples. No one was able to accompany her to the port, not even Manny. He was occupied by his work, and her mother was way too sick to see her off. In no way was Lili going to be the last person Rose would see before she left. So she got on the train to Naples completely on her own.

The ship left around twelve noon. As soon as Rose boarded, she got an upset stomach.

As the ship was leaving the port, she could see all the families and loved ones waving and crying. There was no one there for her. Even though she thought she wouldn't care, she had never felt so alone as she did on this day—no husband, no mother, no sister, no one.

Rose never had any real friends growing up. Her arrogance and vanity did not appeal to many people, causing her to be what she would describe herself, a wallflower. This time, however, her segregation was demoralizing. For the next eleven days until she reached New York, Rose would experience the most reclusive period of her life.

While Rose was departing for America, Lili sat by her mother's bedside. Dahlia knew her time had come, but before she passed on, she had to confess a secret to her daughter, and it was time to tell her.

With her quivering voice barely audible, she began to tell Lili the story of her life—a story that Lili thought she already knew. Dahlia began explaining. She felt it was time Lili knew the truth.

"My precious flower, you know I love you, and your father loved you too, so much." She continued, "It has always been very hard for me to see the way the relationship between you and Rose has developed."

Putting her head down and closing her eyes, Dahlia continued, "I suppose it was our fault for not showing her the same affection we did with you. But we tried our best, and Papa loved her more than *her own* biological father did. He loved both of you so much."

Lili, perplexed, suddenly gasped, "Biological father? Mamma, what are you saying?"

"Please forgive me, cara mia," Dahlia pleaded as the tears began flowing down her face

Dahlia raised her head and began to tell the story. Lili learned that her mother worked as a seamstress in Rome at one time. She was employed at one of the fashion houses belonging to famous designer Elsa Schiaparelli. It was there she met the husband of one of the designer's clients.

Dahlia explained how she was very young at the time, and unfortunately, her naivety threw her right into his arms and his bed. She explained to Lili how he was handsome, sophisticated, and wealthy. Despite the fact he was married, Dahlia fell in love with him. Then one day he disappeared, never to be seen or heard from again.

The tears continued to stream down Dahlia's cheeks. She could barely get the words out. Yet she continued describing her heartbreak and rejection, even from her parents. When she became pregnant, they renounced her and decided to send her to a convent. Impregnated Dahlia was sent to Casa Maria Immaculata in Caserta. Society placed great emphasis on the bonds of marriage, and those who deviated from this social norm faced condemnation from their community. Dahlia's pregnancy had brought shame to her family, which was why her parents sent her away.

The convent was rumored to be one of the Magdalene laundries. These institutions were supposedly for housing "fallen women," a phrase used to imply female sexual promiscuity or those who worked in prostitution. Laundries such as this operated throughout Europe and North America and were named after the Biblical figure Mary Magdalene.

"If it hadn't been for Sister Margherita, I don't know where I would be today," Dahlia claimed. She continued to describe Sister Margherita's compassion and affection for her. This was what saved her. The sister was also responsible for introducing Dahlia to her future husband, Paolo Bianchi. Paolo's aunt was a fellow sister, Sister Agatha. When Margherita heard Agatha's sister had died, leaving behind her only unmarried son, she knew exactly what to do. Paolo was introduced to Dahlia and agreed to marry her.

Lili listened attentively about how Dahlia, at first, was not in love with her husband, but over time, her feelings for Paolo grew. He was a hard worker, good father, loving husband, and not a chauvinist, unlike many men of that period. Once they were married, Paolo decided to take his new bride, Dahlia, and her daughter, Rose, to start a new life in the town of Portici.

"Liliana, get me my storage box from the top shelf." Dahlia pointed to her closet. When Lili handed it over to her mother, Dahlia continued, "Once I go, please promise me you will forever hold on to this. Never let anyone see it, not even your sister."

After Dahlia fell asleep, Lili felt paralyzed. She didn't know what to say or do except stare at her mother for several minutes. Dahlia looked so peaceful at that moment. It was like a heavy burden had been lifted off her shoulders, Lili thought. Yet she was still in a state of shock at what she had learned.

Lili knew that this chest would contain evidence of what her mother had just confessed. While Dahlia slept, Lili made a vow to herself never to betray her mother. As she sat by her bedside, she couldn't help but notice how tranquil Dahlia looked despite the discoloration of her skin and emaciated body. It was at that moment Lili realized it was just a matter of time before her mother would be gone.

What am I going to do? Lili began weeping as she comprehended her upcoming state of solitude. Once her mother passed, she would have no one. Her beloved father was already gone; her sister was starting a whole new life across seas, and now her mother? The only people whom she had any contact with recently were Dottore Conte, the American GI, and Luca. Manny often came around to see how Dahlia was doing. Lili tried to have as little conversation with him as possible. Yet they always managed to divulge in deep dialogue and found commonalities in their convictions and sentiments.

Lili always pondered, *How could he stay back in Portici and send his wife to America without him? The war is over.* Lili tried to analyze his odd conduct, but she couldn't help but also think of Luca. *Oh, Luca, how could my sister let you go when you were so good to her?*

Although Lili spent most of her time taking care of her ailing mother, she would frequently see Luca when she was out to run an errand. He was always so gentle, kind, and attentive when listening to her convey her thoughts and concerns.

Lili had mercy on this heartbroken man, who was still devastated by the rejection of her sister. She knew he was still deeply in love with Rose even though she was now married to a GI and living in America. This was a dream that both Lili and Luca knew Rose had always wished for. They both possessed a mutual understanding of Rose and life in Portici.

Lili always felt safe and secure when conversing with Luca. He seemed to be the only one she could truly confide in other than her mother. How could her sister let go of such a genuine and compassionate man for an arrogant, pretentious, and despicable American?

Of course, Rose could because her American was just like her, Lili tried convincing herself. However, deep down, she knew Manny was nothing like Rose and found herself completely enraptured by him.

As soon as improper thoughts of Manny invaded her mind, Lili would switch over to her mother. She struggled to fall asleep as her mind was consumed with the day behind her, still trying to process what she had learned. Lili's anxiety became too overwhelming.

She wondered if Rose had any inclination about her biological father. Still, Lili would never betray her mother and would keep this secret from everyone. She would do anything to preserve her mother's reputation. People in the village could be so merciless when it came to gossip. It did, however, somewhat change once the war broke out. People were more concerned with surviving than telling tales.

CHAPTER THREE

After a sleepless night, Lili couldn't stay in bed any longer. She felt restless and distressed. She still had so many questions she needed answered. Who was Rose's biological father? Where was he now? Was he aware of his daughter? The only person who could answer these questions was her mother. Lili got up and marched directly to Dahlia's room.

When she entered, she noticed that Dahlia was halfway off her bed.

"Mamma! Mamma!" Lili pleaded while shaking her firmly. A feeling of dread and panic suddenly took over her. "What is happening?" She then realized her beloved mother was dead. She had passed away in her sleep but with no one at her side.

Lili knew the day would come when her mother would die. But why did God take her away now? She whimpered. Her moans quickly turned to hysteria and uncontrollable wailing. In her frenzy, Lili realized she must let someone know, so she called the only person she could think of—Luca. She knew there was nothing he could probably do, but she needed someone comforting, and he was just the person. Even though he could barely understand what she was saying, he knew right away that it was about her mother. As soon as he hung up the telephone, he rushed over to her side. He then contacted the town's physician to come along.

Dottore Vittorio Conte was the local doctor who had treated Dahlia, more so since she became ill. He was someone whom her mother seemed to have much assurance and trust in.

Lili, in hindsight, would recall his many visits. The family knew him their whole lives. Yet he would spend extra time with Dahlia. Not only did he come to treat her, but he would also spend much time talking to her and comforting her. Dahlia and the dottore had a special bond through the years that caused much chatter in the past.

After checking all her vital signs, the dottore pronounced Dahlia dead. As Lili began to sob, Luca placed his arms around her and hugged her tightly. She could barely catch her breath. The news around town began circulating. Many of the neighbors started coming to the apartment to see for themselves.

Where were all these people when we needed them? Lili ruminated as she sat down by her mother's side.

That evening, after all the observers left, Luca asked, "Lilianna, how will you bury your mother?" Lili turned to look at him. He quickly saw the gaze of burden on her face. Everything was happening so quickly, she had not even thought of all this yet.

"Oh dio mio," she choked, "Luca, what do I do?" After reaching for her hands, he held them in his.

Softly he whispered, "I will do whatever I can to help you." Luca continued and suggested that since she could not afford a coffin, he would make one out of Paolo's boat since it had been sitting futile at the port.

It had been so long since Lili had gone back to the boat. As much as she didn't want to part with it, she knew this was a sensible idea. For one, she couldn't afford a coffin, and two, Dahlia could be buried next to her husband, Paolo. He would then have *two* of his eternal loves with him—his wife and his vessel. Luca also offered to transport Dahlia's body to the Cimitero Comunale after the service. It would take place the next day in the apartment itself and would be performed by the local parish priest.

That night, Lili gently washed Dahlia's body with soapy water. She then rubbed a rose-scented balm on her skin and dressed her.

Although Lili was still in a state of mental numbness, she recognized that this was something she had to do out of respect for her mother.

Lili had contemplated dressing Dahlia in her wedding dress; however, she opted for a simple pale-yellow dress instead. She decided that she would keep the bridal gown for herself and one day wear it on her own wedding day. With the help of Luca, they placed small bags of dry ice under Dahlia's hips and shoulders. The following day, about two dozen visitors said their goodbyes to their compatriot. In her serene room lay the bouquet of roses her daughter Rose used for her wedding and a couple of lit candles.

After only one day of viewing, the body of Dahlia was placed in the coffin made from her husband's boat. Lili couldn't believe Luca had made it in only one day. Not only did he build the beautiful coffin, but he also drove his recently purchased Alfa Romeo 430 truck to help transport Dahlia's body to the cemetery. It would only be Lili and Luca accompanying Dahlia to her final resting place. Once there, they would leave the coffin with the groundskeepers for burial.

Seeing Dahlia's coffin next to her father's grave made Lili break down into uncontrollable wails. She had lost everyone. She couldn't bear the thought of where her life would be going now. Her parents were both gone, and her sister was overseas. Everything and everyone in her whole existence seemed to have disintegrated. No one except Luca and Dottore Conte were with her at her most arduous time of need.

Lili did recall how Manny had also been supportive also, but not for long. She knew this situation was peculiar and perilous. There she was, with the two men of her sister, Rose—her previous ex-beau, Luca, and her present husband, Manny. Both were now with Lili, and neither one of them were with Rose.

A couple of days had passed. Although Lili was now living in the apartment alone, she was in the company of someone during these painful days. Neighbors, relatives, and friends of the family were dropping by to make sure the *deserted* Lili had everything she needed. One guest she was not expecting one day was her brother-in-law, Manny.

The doorbell rang, and Lili opened the door. The two of them stared at each other in an astonished gaze for a few seconds.

"Ciao, Lilianna, how are you doing?" Manny addressed softly. Lili lowered her eyes, holding back her tears. He continued, "I just wanted to let you know that I have contacted Rose and given her the news of your mother." Lili didn't even respond to ask how Rose took the news. She knew it wouldn't affect her sister the way it affected her, but she kindly said, "Thank you." She was about to close the door when Manny pushed it back open. "Wait, can I come in?" he pleaded.

"What for?" Lili was startled. Then she continued, "You are my sister's husband. I don't think it would be appropriate."

Manny completely ignored her request and walked in. He then cupped his hands around her face and started kissing her. His hands were in her hair as their tongues, deep in each other's mouths, began a dance of their own. The passion was almost too exhilarating for Lili to handle. Her soul had surrendered to this enemy, and it had expanded into a mysterious euphoria she had never experienced before.

As the kissing intensified, Manny pushed Lili against the wall, pinning her hands up above her head. He lifted her blouse and started to tongue her hardened nipple through the lace bra she wore. She moaned, closing her eyes and allowing the intoxication to overtake her. It was a pleasure so heightened, Lili began to panic. She then pushed him away. But Manny would persist, grabbing her arms and pinning them behind her back.

There was no denying the intense chemistry that had been lingering between them. Manny was so overwhelmed by his desire for her he continued the seduction. He felt himself forcefully ensnaring this beautiful being he had come to crave so fiercely.

Lili was resisting, but the struggle continued. Manny was quickly overcome with guilt and recognized what he was about to do. His conscience would not allow him to continue to take advantage of this virtuous young girl despite his crazed obsession with her. Yet his desire became so intense he could not contain himself. His heart was racing, and his body felt so vigorous; he couldn't stop from kissing and grazing her face, neck, and breasts.

Lili could not deny her own passion for him regardless if he was her sister's husband. Despite her resistance, confusion, and dismay, she felt herself quickly submitting to his coercion. Then she *completely* surrendered to him. She had never felt such intensity, even in her fantasies. This pleasure and euphoria were beyond her recognition. As he ripped open her blouse and tore at her bra to expose her breasts, he took one nipple into his mouth and started caressing and twisting the other one with his fingers. As he went from breast to breast, Lili felt the moistness between her legs drench her panties.

Her sweet and soft moans were more than Manny could manage. He wanted to ejaculate right then and there but longed for his penis to feel her wet and tight vagina. He started kissing her down her stomach then lifted her skirt and pulled down her panties. As he started to kiss and lick her soft, pure vulva, he inserted a finger and gently began to penetrate.

Manny's elation escalated as her moans of pleasure increased. He just couldn't wait another moment to have intercourse. He quickly exposed his hard, enlarged penis and inserted it into Lili. He raised her arms above her head and kissed her intensely.

As Lili felt his penis enter her, she experienced a pain like never before. It was a perplexing paradox of pleasure and pain. Her legs quivered as he lifted and carried her to the bed. His penis never exited her vagina. Manny ejaculated quicker than he had anticipated. He hoped she didn't recognize the hastiness since she was still a virgin.

Lili was bewildered. As he held her face and gently kissed her lips, she began to cry. Manny stood up and took her hands into his, raising her from the bed. Her tears continued to roll down her cheeks. He grabbed her arms and placed his arms around her, hugging her so tight she almost felt suffocated.

"Please forgive me," he whispered into her ear. He then kissed her cheek. Manny was so overcome with emotions; he, too, began to cry. Lili was baffled by this man's sentiment but was not sure if it was because he was overwhelmed with guilt or that he really did have genuine feelings for her.

When Lili unraveled from the hug, she noticed the bloodstains on the bed.

"Oh dio!" She was mortified. "How could I do this?" she blurted. "I ruined my mother's bed! The very bed she died in a few days ago! There is blood everywhere! How could you do this to me?" she hollered.

"I'm sorry, Lilianna, but I love you!" As Manny noticed Lili's eye widen from the shock of what she just heard, he continued, "Yes, you heard me correctly. I love you. I know I married your sister, but it is you I love."

Lili placed her hands on Manny's chest to push him away.

"Please go! Just please leave, and go back to America where you belong with your wife!"

"But I can't go! I need you, Lili!" Manny pleaded.

"You have to, Manny. There is no place for you here. Please go!" As Lili began to cry once again, Manny realized she was right. There was nothing he could do now. He had no choice but to leave and forget her and Italy.

As Manny walked out the door, Lili could feel her heart beating rapidly and her body shake. She couldn't stop staring at the blood-stained sheets they had just soiled. How could she do this? Lili was distressed. Not only did she have sex for the first time and lost her virginity, but it was with her sister's husband.

"Oh dio, what would Rose do if she ever found out about this liaison?" Rose already detested her younger sister for so many reasons, but now this. Lili realized she had to erase this incident from her memory. No one was to ever know, and she would never speak or think of it again.

Lili quickly gathered the sheets to soak them in bleach. Her mind and body were still flustered by the incident. She walked to the kitchen and left the sheets soaking in the bathtub. Then there was a knock at the door.

Please don't let it be him again. Lili was afraid, but after carefully opening it, she breathed a sigh of relief.

"Luca, I am so happy to see you."

Puzzled by her greeting, Luca quickly inquired, "Was that *the American* I saw leaving here?"

"Yes," she fretted.

"What did he need?" Luca asked sternly.

"He came by to only tell me he informed Rose of our mother's death," Lili explained nervously.

"Ahhhhh, okay." Luca hesitated for a while then continued, "Lilianna," as he took her hands, "I am here for another reason. I have something I want to ask you."

Still feeling weary of what had just occurred with Manny, Lili released her hands from Luca. She walked over to sit on the sofa in the parlor. Once she sat down, Luca knelt in front of her and took her hands once again.

"Lili, you know I am very fond of you. We have so much in common."

Without hesitation, Lili blurted, "Yes, my sister!" Luca was taken aback by her sarcastic remark. However, he had always been aware of their rift and especially how much Rose despised Lili.

After pausing for a few seconds, Luca carried on.

"I'm not referring to your sister. I don't even want to talk about her anymore. She is out of my life and yours! I'm here to discuss us." Lili was startled and stared at him with bewilderment. What was he talking about? "I think we should get married!" Luca suddenly uttered.

"What?" Lili was so stunned by his request she started to mumble. She did not make any sense in her muttering.

Luca shook her and said, "Lili, you are alone now, and I am alone. We know each other so well, and yes, I did love your sister—*once*. But I need *you* in my life. You are who I want to marry. It's not because I don't have Rose, or I could marry someone else. But I want to be with you, and I know we can be happy together." Lili felt overpowered. The irony of having both of her sister's men in one day was insane. She had passionate sex with one who confessed his love for her. The other one was now asking for her hand in marriage.

Lili's shock quickly turned to interest. This was actually a good idea, she thought. She was alone, and Luca was a wonderful man. Plus she needed to get Manny out of her mind. This was the perfect arrangement. Yes, he was once her sister's beau. Yes, she was aware that Rose had sex with Luca many times. Yet the thought of it did not make her feel uneasy. This was not about sex. It was about a shared admiration they had for each other.

They were not *in love*, but there was an unspoken adoration based on mutual respect and fondness. This could assure a stable marriage. Lili decided to sleep on her decision before accepting Luca's proposal but had already made up her mind. She didn't want to come across too eager and desperate, so she would wait until the next day to give him her agreement.

After sleeping alone in the empty apartment, Lili had no doubts regarding her decision. The next day, Luca returned, and much to his excitement, Lili accepted his suggestion. It had only been five days since her mother's death, but her desolation was becoming overwhelming. At first, she had thought she would wait until at least a month after her mother's demise. However, she just couldn't wait any longer. Thus, Lili and Luca planned to be married as soon as possible.

There would only be a church service. Portici was in ruins, and neither one of them had any money for a reception. Unlike Rose and Manny, Lili and Luca would wed at the Rettoria Dell'Immacolata a Cappella Reale church. Lili would also wear her beloved mother's bridal gown, a dress she held so dear to her heart, not only because Dahlia wore it on her wedding day but also because her mother made the dress herself. The very gown Rose opposed for her wedding on account of it being outdated, Lili felt privileged and appreciative to wear, especially in honor of her deceased mother.

Dahlia had hand sewn the gown herself, and although it was many years old, it was a beautiful masterpiece of her mother's talent. Lili had always been fascinated with the 1920s. That era was all about decadence and swinging silhouettes. They were inspired by bold art deco patterns, jazz music, and Egyptian motifs (thanks to the discovery of King Tut's tomb). The gown was an ivory silk chiffon dress with beading and sequins, sparkling embroidery, and exquisite detailing, with a drop waist and a wedding slip underneath.

One week after the death of her mother, Lili, dressed in Dahlia's masterpiece, became a wife. She was now Mrs. Luca Marchese. Although she still could not get Manny out of her mind, she vowed to focus on her marriage to her new husband.

Lili needed know how her mother passed and was determined to find out what killed her. What was it that had caused Dahlia to become so ill and die? Lili was fully aware of all the illness and diseases brought upon by the war, but no one could give her any candid explanation about her mother, not even Dottore Conte.

After the ceremony, Lili helped Luca unpack his belongings at the apartment. She had focused so much on the marriage that she had not given any thought to the wedding night. Now, realizing they would need to consummate the marriage, Lili became enormously nervous and frightened. Luca was an incredibly handsome man, but she was not in love with him. How could she have sex with him less than a couple of days after having sex with his nemesis? Lili horrifically realized she would be having sex with both of her sister's men.

Oh dio! Lili grimaced. *What is happening to me?* The tears began to stream down her face uncontrollably as she sat down on her mother's bed. When Luca asked her what was wrong, she simply stated she missed her mother. Although this was mostly true, she still couldn't grapple with the sudden turn of events.

In one week, Lili had lost her mother, had sex with her brother-in-law, and married her sister's ex-lover. Rose was always the defiant sibling—bold, brash, and did what she wanted without guilt or shame. Lili was considered the ever-so-sweet and innocent sister whom everyone praised for being the honest and virtuous. Yet she was the one who had committed more mortal sins.

Rose was so envious and resentful of her especially for these very reasons. Lili began to analyze the circumstances. At first, she fretted but then began to develop a twist of emotions. Why should she always be so mindful and cognizant of others, especially Rose?

The two most important people in her life—her mother and father—were now gone. Her sister was overseas and had no interest in what was happening back in Portici. Manny was leaving for the United States, and she would probably never see him again.

Lili quickly concluded that no one really cared except Luca. After going through such a devastating war, most people only attended to their own needs of survival. It was a tumultuous time, and the war had destroyed people's souls—a battle that had starved, dehumanized, and killed millions. At the end of it, Lili was just another innocent victim. Without her family, she would remain a desolate and lonesome young woman. She was just another casualty of war.

All her life, Lili had protected and maintained her virtue. Perhaps it was time she emerged from this prison of righteousness. She needed to become selfish and merciless. After pondering all these uncharacteristic thoughts, Lili decided one day she would have the courage to alter her character. However, for now, her concentration and determination were to uncover the cause of her mother's death.

"Are you tired, my love?" Luca inquired.

My love? That was the first time any man referred to her as *his love*. As strange as it sounded, Lili liked the sound of it. "Yes, a little." She sighed.

"Then come to bed, my wife." Luca grinned proudly. As he picked her up by her hands off the chair, Lili became increasingly nervous. She knew exactly what was about to transpire in the bedroom.

As Luca began to kiss her, Lili realized this was the first time they had ever kissed. It was a very passionate and sensual kiss, yet her mind quickly turned to thoughts of Manny. How much she longed for his kiss, his touch, and wished it was him she was about to have sex with again instead of Luca.

Did her strong feelings for Manny compel her to fantasize about *him* right now? Or was it because she was aware of Luca's shortcomings when it came to his sexuality that she was so apprehensive? She often pitied Luca when Rose would rant about his sexual inabilities.

Although Rose and Lili were never close and never discussed intimate details, Rose always felt the need to expose poor Luca's sexual defect often. Lili would be disgusted with her sister for expressing these private matters. Luca was her husband, and she vowed to never disrespect him the way Rose did.

Luca slowly took off her clothes and his. They began to make love on the very bed she and Manny had sex just days ago. Although the marriage was now being consummated, Luca did not ejaculate, and Lili never became aroused.

This was not the intense, lewd, and erotic sex she had experienced with Manny. How she yearned for him right now. Her body had never known such pleasure, yet her heart had never known such pain. The thought of him going back to America to Rose was a reality Lili wasn't sure she would be able to accept. However, she realized she had no choice. It was her choice, after all, to marry Luca. She could have had Manny if she wanted. He had even confessed his love to her, but Lili did what she felt was best for everyone.

Luca awoke to find Lili already out of the bed. He sat up on the edge of the bed and started to look around him. He groaned. Lili was not a virgin. There were no bloodstains on the sheets. Who was the one who took his sweet Lili's purity away at sixteen years of age? While standing in the shower, Luca became more and more disturbed by the idea of his new wife having had sex with someone else. He decided to find a distraction. He needed to get to the bottom of this.

"Lilianna, I will go to my home to get the rest of my belongings," he muttered.

Lili, puzzled by his strange tone, simply nodded as he walked out the door. When she sat down at the kitchen table to reflect on the last few days, there was a knock on the door.

"Buon giorno, Lili." It was Manny.

Lili, looking at him, stunned, suddenly blurted, "What are you doing here?"

"I came to see you!" he proclaimed.

"You must leave, Manny. You must!" she continued frantically. "No one can see you here, especially my husband!"

Did she just say "my husband"? Manny, horrified by what he had just heard, froze. At that moment, he didn't know what to say. He felt like his world had just crumbled around him. The thought of another man sleeping in her bed nauseated him. This young woman had just wounded him beyond anything he had ever experienced, even combat.

After a few seconds of silence, Manny frantically asked, "You are married?"

As the tears began to stream down Lili's face, she lowered her eyes and quietly answered, "Yes."

"Who is he?" Manny demanded. "Who is this husband of yours?"

"It's Luca Marchese." Lili looked up at Manny's eyes. They widened with a stare of disgust and terror.

"Luca? Rose's Luca?" shrieked Manny.

"He is not Rose's anything now. He's my husband! And you are Rose's husband! Now please go away!" Lili demanded. When she closed the door, Manny put his foot against it. He clenched his hands into a fist but quickly realized there was nothing he could do at this point.

Lili was able to finally close the door. She began to cry hysterically and fell to the floor.

Manny felt sickened to his stomach as he stormed out of the shattered old building. He crouched over, gagging, feeling like he was about to vomit.

Manny could barely walk. He felt like an empty shell. He slowly walked across the street, disoriented, when Luca approached the building and spotted him.

What is he doing here again? he fumed. *Was he the one that took Lili's virginity?* An alarming sensation overtook Luca.

With her face in her hands and her torso swaying back and forth, Lili heard the door swung open. Was it Manny again? She gulped.

Before she could get up and turn around, Luca screeched, "Lili, what is wrong? Why are you on the floor like that? What did that bastard say to you?"

Lili tried to get herself up off the floor but began to panic. She knew right away Luca had seen Manny leaving the building. After composing herself, she stressed, "He was here simply to say goodbye and ask if I needed anything to be sent to Rose before he left."

"Then why are you crying like this?" Luca asked suspiciously.

"How can you ask me this after everything that has happened to me lately? You are the only family I have left, Luca." When guilt began to alter his mood, he embraced his new wife and kissed her on the forehead.

To quickly change the subject, Lilly sniffled, "I must call Dottore Conte!"

"Why do you need to call him? Are you all right, my love?" Luca questioned.

"No! I will never be all right until I know what killed my mother!" Lili fumed. "The Dottore is fully aware, and I know he and my mother were hiding something!"

As she dialed the doctor's number, Luca became muddled by Lili's sudden change in demeanor. She was displaying a much more tenacious side of herself, one he had never noticed she possessed. Was being married now bringing out more mature or grittier qualities in her? His tension intensified when he watched and listened to his wife take command of the telephone.

"Dottore! I must see you at once!" she demanded.

"What is the problem, my dear? Are you not feeling well?" The dottore worried.

"No. I am not! Please come to me as soon as possible!" Lili didn't tell him the real reason she wanted to see him. She feared it would make him hesitate to visit.

Dottore Conte was at Lili's front door within fifteen minutes. He always had a special spot in his heart for her, and knowing she had been left alone was truly disheartening for him.

"Lilianna, what's wrong?" he asked, noticing she actually looked well when she answered the door. Dottore Conte was surprised to see a familiar man walking toward him when he walked in.

"Ciao, Dottore," greeted Luca, extending his hand to shake the doctor's.

"Luca?"

"Yes. Please forgive my wife for disturbing you." Just as the doctor turned to Lili, a look of astonishment came over his face.

"Your wife?"

"Yes, Dottore. Luca and I were married yesterday," Lili quickly interjected.

"My congratulations to both of you. Now tell me. Why am I here?" By the tone of his voice, Luca realized the dottore had become a little agitated, so he quickly excused himself and left him and Lili alone. "Lilianna! What is this all about? You said you were not well! Yet you seem perfectly fine to me! And you just got married? What is going on here?"

"This is not about my marriage, Dottore, or about me. It's about my mother."

"Your mother? What about Dahlia? That poor soul is in eternal rest. Let her rest in peace," he begged.

"I will never rest until I know why she died!" Lili snapped.

"I understand, my little flower, but you know war has brought upon much illness. Unfortunately, your mother succumbed to one."

"What illness?" she demanded. With a scowl on her face like no one had seen before, especially the doctor, she continued, "You will tell me immediately how my mother died!"

Dottore Conte knew it was not ethical to disclose medical information. After removing his fedora hat, he sat down and began to cry. Lili was puzzled and disturbed.

"Oh dio, why are you crying?" Was he in love with her mother? Was this why he was crying? After all, he was visiting her quite often while she was alive, and they were always in private.

"Please just tell me what killed her. Please! I beg you. Why did both of you always keep secrets? So many people have passed from so many diseases and the war, yet every time I asked, neither of you would give me a straight answer. Why? What was so unusual about her death that no one could tell me exactly what it was?" Lili implored. Dottore Conte, still weeping, looked up at her and realized it was time she knew the truth.

CHAPTER FOUR

"Lilianna, sit down, please." Lili sat and noticed the look on his face, one of anguish and guilt. "I want you to hear this from me before the townspeople start talking and stun you with rumors. You don't deserve to be deceived like this, and now that I see you are married, I would suggest you and Luca start a new life elsewhere."

Lili became quite concerned but couldn't understand where this rambling about deception was going. All she wanted to know was how her mother died. Malaria? Tuberculosis? She was fully aware of the impact the war had on the world. Millions of people were dead from combat, diseases, and illness. But unlike her father's death from the bombing, Dahlia's demise seemed inexplicable.

"Your mother's death was caused by syphilis," the doctor candidly stated. Lilly sank to the ground and fell on her knees. Did she just hear him right? She may have been young, but she knew all too well what the disease was. Syphilis was one of the many war-related epidemics causing deaths during that war. However, the difference with this condition, as opposed to the others, was that this was a sexually transmitted disease. How could this be possible? Her father was dead for over a year. Was it from him that Dahlia contracted this disease? If so, that would mean he had been with other women. If not, her mother had been with other men.

Lili was too shocked to know what to do next. She then got up off her knees and stood up. With a look of complete disgust, she demanded, "How could my mother possibly die from syphilis?"

Dottore Conte didn't know what to say other than, "Lilianna, you wanted to know how your mother died, and I told you. I will not be responsible for anything further. Now if you will excuse me, I have other appointments to tend to."

As the doctor walked out the door, Lili became sickened. She fell to her knees once again and began to vomit on the cold, hard cement floor. The arc of her life and heroine's image was altered in an instant. Suddenly, the present made no sense, and the future seemed impossible to imagine. In such a short time, she had discovered her sister, Rose, was fathered by another man, and her mother died of a sexually transmitted disease. In addition, she had sexual relations with her sister's husband and married her sister's ex-lover.

After composing herself and cleaning the floor, she sat down at the kitchen table. She began to cry uncontrollably. What could she possibly do now? Was it her beloved father who infected her mother over a year ago? Was it her mother who was infected by someone else? Although she knew that either way, the outcome would be painful, she was determined to find out the truth behind her mother's demise.

When Luca returned a short time after, he found Lili sitting at the kitchen table, crying again.

"Lilianna, what's wrong now?"

Wiping her tears while looking up at him, she muttered quietly, "There is something I must do." When he approached the table and sat down next to her, she continued, "I need you to take me somewhere."

"Where do you need to go, my love?" Luca questioned.

"Caserta," she stated. Looking clueless and baffled, Luca sat up in his chair.

"Caserta? What for? What do you need to do there?" he yelped.

"If you don't want to take me there, I will find my own way!" Lili exploded.

Here was that tenacious side of her that Luca was noticing lately. Lili's disposition was altering. Without a moment more of hesitation, he responded, "Yes, of course I will take you, but please just tell me why."

"I need to see Sister Margherita at Casa Maria Immaculata in Caserta!" Lilly commanded.

With his hands on his hips, still looking confused, Luca questioned, "Who is that? Why do you need to see a nun?"

Lili stressed, "She was like a mother to my mother. I have questions I need answered! Understand?"

While Lili was exasperated, Luca was getting more and more rattled. For so long, she was this young, sweet, and innocent blossom. Now she was becoming a wilted flower. Luca could understand how hard it must have been for his new bride. To be dealing with so much so suddenly was excruciating. Yet her behavior was beginning to worry him.

Up until Dahlia could not leave her home any longer, she would frequently make trips up to Caserta to see Sister Margherita. From the moment they met many years ago, when Dahlia was pregnant with Rose, Margherita had become Dahlia's companion, adviser, and mentor. Lili knew her mother confided in the sister for many years and wanted to finally meet her. She also required answers regarding her mother's past.

The following day, Lili and Luca began the forty-minute drive from Portici to Caserta. For most of the drive, not much was uttered between them. Luca would glance over periodically, only to see the tears streaming down his wife's face while she stared out of the window. When they finally reached the convent, Lili jumped out before the vehicle had come to a complete stop. Luca began to shout, "Lilianna!" but she was already at the front doorway.

The monastery was a grandiose villa with majestic handcrafted mahogany entry doors. Lili banged on the metal doorknocker so hard, it echoed throughout the grounds. After Lili knocked several times, two nuns opened the doors. After seeing the weeping angelic young girl, their scowls quickly turned to concern.

"My child, what brings you here to us?" one of them asked.

"Please, I need Sister Margherita!" begged Lili.

After going back into the convent, one of the nuns turned to walk away. As she made her way down the corridor, the other one wrapped her arm around Lili's shoulders.

"Now, now, my child, everything will be all right. Sister Magdalena will bring Sister Margherita to you."

Continuing to weep, Lili promptly saw Sister Magdalena walking back with another sister alongside her. When she realized this was probably Sister Margherita, a sigh of relief came upon her. The sister's face had a look of interest as she stared at Lili.

"I am Dahlia Bianchi's daughter," Lili declared once they approached her. Sister Margherita still looked confused, and then Lili remembered the sister would recognize Dahlia by her maiden name. "Dahlia Rossi." Sister Margherita suddenly began to cry.

"Oh my! She has passed, hasn't she?"

"Yes, sister." As Lili continued to sob, Sister Margherita took her by the arm and guided her to a small chapel not far from the entrance.

When they both sat down in one of the chapel pews, Lili didn't hesitate.

"Sister? Please tell me the truth about my mother."

"What truth might that be, my dear child?" Margherita looked at Lili's face of despair.

"Mamma told me the truth about my sister and how her father is a different man from mine." As Sister Margherita listened to Lili explain what Dahlia had confessed to her, she realized Lili was not informed about *everything*.

Sister Margherita was contemplating whether to tell Lili more but acknowledged the consequences that would arise. However, when Lili informed her of Dottore Conte's statement concerning the townspeople stunning her with rumors, the sister sympathized tremendously. She believed that although this was a conflict of interest, she would justify some of Dahlia's life and hardships.

Uncertain of what Lili's reactions would be with the information, Sister Margherita slowly, carefully, and sensitively began to reveal some details of Dahlia's secrets. Sister Margherita had known Dahlia for the last twenty-five years, and Lili knew that the sister was her mother's confidant all these years.

Rose's biological father was a man named Alberto Mancini, an Italian jewelry designer, businessman, and nobleman living in Rome. He was a descendant of one of the oldest aristocratic families of Roman nobility. Their titles and fiefs were numerous, and the family was also granted the Honneurs de la Cour of France. The Palazzo Mancini in Rome was the second home of the French Academy from 1737 to 1793. Dahlia had fallen deeply in love with this man, but he was married. His wife, Cecilia, was a well-known socialite who was an avid art collector and style icon. No wonder Rose was cold-blooded, Lili thought to herself; she came from blue blood. If Rose ever found out, she would be even more egocentric than she already was.

Sister Margherita continued to explain why Dahlia's parents made the decision to send her to the convent. They determined that sending Dahlia to the convent was a far lesser punishment then having to deal with Alberto's family and associates. Had the truth been revealed, the consequences would have been severe.

"Is he still in Rome, Sister?" Lili asked.

"I'm not sure, my child. But I remember hearing he might have relocated to Milan."

"Okay, please continue," Lilly pleaded.

"My child, you must forgive your mother for her past mistakes." Sister Margherita urged, "She did the best she could, and she loved all of you very much. Paolo was an admirable man who loved Dahlia with all his heart. Had he still been alive, he would have even forgiven her for her *trading activities*. He would have completely understood she was doing it to feed her family."

"Trading activities?" At that moment, Sister Margherita noticed the look of complete shock on Lili's face. She believed Lili was already aware of her mother's actions considering she had died from syphilis.

"Oh dio!" The sister didn't know what to say next. Should she tell Lili the truth? Sister Margherita knew that once Lili discovered *more* of her mother's secrets, it would be devastating. However, to protect her from traumatic gossip, Margherita continued to reveal more information.

What Lili had discovered about her mother was more than traumatic. How was this even possible? For the past couple of years, Dahlia had been prostituting herself. Her lovely, virtuous, beloved mother was working as a whore.

When she was supposedly working as a seamstress, she was having sex. Lili was appalled and had to hold back from heaving. After reflecting for a moment, she recalled that her mother's clients were *mostly* men.

Poverty in Italy was legendary in its proportions, and war conditions pushed this to further extremes. Many without ready access to food did almost anything to survive. Hunger governed everything, and the people had witnessed moral collapse. There was no more pride nor dignity. At the cost of any corruption or depravity, food was the only thing that mattered. Naples and its surrounding areas experienced what was called total defeat. The bombing contributed to the mass disorganization and chaos of society. It was these forces that drove so many women to prostitute themselves.

While officially, commanders supported the US War Department's prohibition of prostitution, in private, they normalized it and even encouraged sexual avenues. This was necessary to maintain troop morale.

There was an estimated female population of over 150,000 in the Naples area alone. Many of them became freelance whores. This compounded the problems caused by the estimated 50,000 regular prostitutes already. Many of the brothels had previously been regulated by the civilian government and used by the German and Italian Armies.

The 1940s was a tumultuous time, and war had destroyed people's souls. While most people focused on the physical injuries, it was the invisible injuries that would take a lifetime to heal and would affect the lives of generations to come.

While Sister Margherita was speaking, Lili's mind would flash back to so many daunting memories. She recalled how often it was freezing, and crying babies were everywhere. People were being bitten by huge rats. There was so much sickness, drunkenness, and death.

Lili often had terrible nightmares. Still afraid of the dark, she always slept with a little night-light on. By the end of the war, Lili and her family were hungry and innocent victims of a harrowing and agonizing battle. The country was in ruins, the economy had collapsed, and people were eating rations handed out by troops.

Although the Napolitano people were happy to be liberated, the Allies did not have the resources to do much. People became desperate for food, and the black market flourished. Many ordinary women, including housewives, had turned to prostitution out of despair, including Dahlia.

Lilianna was in a complete state of dismay after hearing all this. The thought of her beloved mother exchanging sexual acts for money and food was a concept she could not grasp. Why would Sister Margherita disclose all these details to her? Why? Lilly collapsed in complete anguish, screaming and wailing powerfully; Luca could hear it outside.

Troubled by what he was detecting, Luca immediately ran to the front doors. He began thumping the heavy door knocker so loudly, his knocks echoed even louder than those of Lili's and became deafening. When one of the sisters opened the door, Luca ran past her without hesitation and started yelling out Lili's name. Within seconds, he noticed his frail wife sitting in the little chapel to his left. Lili arose from her seat and ran into his arms after he ran in. They embraced tightly, then Luca demanded, "Lilianna! What is going on here?" When he looked over at Sister Margherita, she noticed the look of panic and confusion on his face.

"Please forgive me, Lord." Margherita sniffed as she tried to hold back her own tears. After doing the sign of the cross, she turned to them. "Lilianna, just before your mother passed, she came to see me one last time. She knew you would come to me and ask questions. Dahlia asked me to promise I would tell you this." Sister Margherita continued, "Although your mother worried you would possibly detest her for all these lies, she would never rest in peace knowing she had deceived you."

Margherita also pleaded that they both leave the town of Portici and begin a new life elsewhere, just as Dottore Conte had advised. Lili, still sobbing, turned to her and gave her a tight hug.

Why am I hugging her? she thought to herself. The sister had just exposed her mother's darkest secrets. Nonetheless, she was Dahlia's surrogate mother and thus her grandmother.

Discovering all this shocking information regarding her beloved mother was like being hit by a bolt of lightning. With all this inconceivable information, this woman had just completely shattered Lili's world. Yet Lili finally realized that Sister Margherita deeply loved and cared for Dahlia and was sparing Lili from future shameful taunts and deception. Furthermore, it was Dahlia who had requested that her secrets be revealed and justified to her daughter.

As Lili and Luca drove away, Sister Margherita stood at the doorway and began to cry profusely. Her intention was never to harm this blameless girl who had come to visit with her. She did it for her love of Dahlia and respected her wishes to tell Lili what was requested of her.

The drive up to the convent was a silent commute, with barely any words muttered between Lili and Luca. However, the drive back would be filled with continuous, rapid conversing as Lili explained everything to Luca about what Sister Margherita had disclosed.

Lili trusted Luca more than anyone. He was the only one she had left in her life. Although stunned and speechless, Luca listened attentively to everything his wife had uncovered. Rose and Lili had different fathers. They were distinctive flowers that fate bloomed in the same garden.

Lili shifted her story from Rose having a different father to the revelation of Dahlia prostitution and how she ultimately died from Syphilis. This came as no surprise to Luca. Rumors had been circulating about the prostitutes, the black market, and corruption among the town. Regular housewives were leading a new class of women into prostitution, making the common whore more difficult to characterize. Italian women were viewed as aggressors and agents of infection by the soldiers. Because they were thought of as shameless and belligerent, these women were demonized as sirens that created sexual demand in order to cash in.

Such women were naive about health matters. They did not take precautions, and as a result, a great percentage of them became sick, such as Dahlia. However, GIs were exonerated from any responsibility in spreading venereal infection. The soldiers were considered hapless victims of the Italian women, unable to resist aroused sexual desires, especially from a woman such as Dahlia who was considered a beautiful, buxom woman most men couldn't resist.

Venereal disease symbolized fragility of masculinity, and this symbol of weakness compromised this masculinity. Many soldiers found condoms more useful to cover their rifle barrels to keep mud out than they did for protection. Soldiers were warned that "your carelessness is their secret weapon," and venereal diseases were called "the enemy in your pants."

Naples had become the largest rest camp for Allied servicemen in all liberated Europe. It was considered the worst governed city in the world; it grew to become the main testing ground of American Italian relations. Neapolitans no longer had decency and morality. Their struggles and hunger dominated everything.

Lili knew that there had become an irrational, deep-rooted aspect of Neapolitans, in general of Southern Italians. Their mentality had forced them to survive on prostitution, thievery, and a desperate belief in miracles and cures. Nevertheless, she would have never imagined her own mother falling prey to the lowest level of shame.

Dahlia was stylish, good-looking, and well-endowed, in which her daughter could relate. People always compared the two and often joked about Lili being Dahlia's clone. The beauty possessed by both mother and daughter caused much jealousy among the women of the town, especially for Rose. Neither of them was very sociable or talkative, yet this didn't stop the women from chattering.

While sitting on her bed, reflecting, Lili realized it was her mother's indiscretions that were the real reason behind the gossip, not her beauty. How did she not ever notice her own mother's misconduct? Southern Italy, and especially Naples, was notorious for prostitution. The people always joked about how the soldiers could not resist the seductive sirens of Naples.

For the last five years, Lilianna had known only war. Together with her sister, Rose; mother, Dahlia; and father, Paolo, she had watched one gruesome spectacle after another from the balcony of their squalid little apartment. It was only once the Allied Forces liberated Italy when they found some solace. It was then that Lili would start frequenting her father's crippled fishing boat, left at the port, to obtain comfort.

During the last few years, Lili had witnessed so many atrocities. Death, hunger, and desperation were evident every moment of every day. The lives of a once proud and vibrant people were now buried in a sea of corruption. Their strong religious beliefs had always guided their behavior in previous years. However, men were now urinating anywhere regardless of women being about. Most children were barefoot and dirty as soap was next to food for its shortage. Of course, there were the prostitutes. The problem was that they were not just whores but common women who were so desperate. They did not enter prostitution by choice but rather out of necessity.

Perhaps Lili could find some relief in knowing that her beloved mother did what she did simply for survival. In the last year, since Paolo's death, Lili truly expressed a painful resentment toward life. Her country was destroyed and in ruins. She had lost both her parents. Even Rose was gone and now living in America. Although she had never had a real connection with her older sister, discovering she was only a half sibling quickly disconnected their minimal bond.

The revelations regarding her mother's past were beyond Lili's comprehension. How much more agony could anyone endure? There were moments when she wondered why God didn't take her too, to spare her from all this anguish and suffering.

Lili was with Luca now, the man she could begin a whole new life with. No sooner did that notion appear in her mind that she burst into tears and somehow muttered, "Manny!" Luca heard something come from his wife's voice, including her sobbing. He approached her, then Lili panicked, realizing he had heard her. After entering the room, Lili shouted, "Mommy!' pretending it was this she had blurted instead of Manny's name. As she began to tremble, Luca sat down beside her and hugged her tighter than ever.

Oh, thank God. She sighed in relief. When he kissed her forehead, she knew he didn't hear correctly the first time.

"Lilianna, we must leave this place as soon as possible." She looked up at him with confusion. He continued, "You heard Sister Margherita and Dottore Conte. We must move away. My zia Emma, who lives in Avellino, has offered us her empty home in Benevento."

Luca barely finished the sentence when Lili shouted, "Yes!" At that moment, she felt embarrassed for having sounded so excited during a time of such sorrow. Yet she knew this would be the best direction in life for both of them.

Without hesitation, Lili and Luca gathered all their belongings and pulled away from their cherished yet ruined town of Portici. Without telling anyone in the town, they began their two-hour journey to the city of Benevento. Although the city was also damaged by the air raids and devastated by earthquakes, it was still able to preserve many of its historic buildings. It did not experience the level of devastation as did Naples and its surrounding towns such as Portici.

Luca was satisfied knowing he had finally brought a fragment of happiness to his wife. Lili, however, had only one element constantly running through her mind—Manuele Catalano. She tried so hard to distract her thoughts of him, but her desire outweighed all other factors.

"How do I stop loving you?" murmured Lili.

The thought of Rose sharing his bed and living with him brought her great anxiety. Lili began to feel tired and sick. Her vomiting forced Luca to stop a few times along the way. What he regarded as uneasiness toward a new move was Lili's discontent due to her thoughts of Manny.

When they finally arrived in Benevento, Lili was astonished at the size of their new home. It was a centuries-old two-level mini *palazzo*. By some miracle, most of the buildings had not been completely destroyed. They were, however, surrounded by debris and rubble, which were evidence of the bomb raids that had taken place in recent years. Many of the city's historic buildings were centuries-old staples of the town, and their little *palazzo*, although slightly disabled, was still in adequate condition.

Because of her strong faith and religious dedication, Lili believed this was a sign—a sign from God that this would be her home and that she and Luca were meant to be together in this house "saved" by God.

As they unloaded their belongings, Lili surveyed the house. A sense of serenity and stability came over her. This was it. After everything that had happened in her life, Lili finally felt like this was her compensation for a lifelong struggle with pain and suffering.

As she reflected on the events leading up to this day, she still couldn't keep Manny out of her mind. Why was this man consuming her every thought, her every emotion every moment of every day? He was Rose's husband. She had her own husband now, Luca. But he, too, had been with Rose first.

"Oh dio!" She winced. Most of her life, it was evident that her older sister was jealous of her. Now, in a twist of developments, Lili found herself envious and bothered by Rose.

For the first time in her life, Lili sensed the rivalry that had escalated between the two of them. Lili had always experienced frightening venom living under the same roof as Rose. She would always maintain the natural state of a sibling relationship. But why did she try so hard with someone who only kept diminishing this affiliation?

It was evident to Lili, more than ever, that Rose had no intention of *ever* establishing a rapport with her. She was far too selfish and egotistic to ever back down. Lili's love and respect for Rose had dwindled. It was Rose's behavior that forced Lili to have these feelings of defiance, wanting to turn the tables.

As Lili pondered over her change of emotions, a devilish smirk came across her face. It was a smirk that Luca noticed as soon as he walked in.

"I'm glad to see you smile." He grinned. If only he knew why, she worried. Her thoughts were on Manny, the man she truly loved, and Rose, the sister who loathed her from the very first day.

When Lili was born, Rose was jealous and angry at no longer being the only child. Rose always persecuted Lili relentlessly throughout their childhood. Lili's bitterness in life was due not only to a few years of war but a lifetime of an abhorrent, damaging rivalry. With the loss of both her parents, she realized it would leave her damaged to a point that would forever affect her happiness.

Rose always seemed to revel in the divide. Yet what would Rose do if she ever found out about her liaisons with Luca and Manny? Lili had no doubt this would probably send Rose over the edge. Most people painted Lili with the same brush, as virtuous and wholesome. Perhaps it was time Lili removed her halo and wings and become the dangerous demoness Lilith Rose had labeled her.

Was she really a dangerous demoness? Someone who represented chaos, seduction, and ungodliness? After all, she had violated most of her moral principles. Lili had sex with Manny, Rose's husband, and married Luca, Rose's ex-lover. Her faith and love for God, however, would never waiver. But she was wretched and broken, and the fabric of her being was now tarnished by all these sins.

CHAPTER FIVE

When the USAHS *Algonquin* steamed into New York Harbor, the only sight that thrilled Rose was the Statue of Liberty. Her American husband had unusually been delayed in Italy. He was not able to greet his new bride when she arrived. Furthermore, the war brides were all kept on the boat for another four days to take care of all the necessary shots and interrogation.

The newly arrived brides did get one day to see the city with a bus. Rose was astounded by the city sights, especially the Automat. It was a fast-food restaurant where simple foods and drinks were served by vending machines. She would just stare at all the little glass compartments with all the different variety of foods. After being hungry for so many years during the war, this was truly fascinating for Rose. But here she was, weeks after her marriage, alone, arriving in *his* country, and observing a whole new world.

After the fantasy of the skyscrapers and the Statue of Liberty, Rose was quickly back to reality. She became nervous after seeing swarms of grumpy officials checking passports, medical reports, and luggage. Above all, she was irritable at having to state the name of a husband or of whoever was going to meet her at the ship. No one could leave until such a person had arrived, and she wasn't sure who was coming for her. She had brought a dome-topped trunk and was ordered to paint her name beforehand on the outside in large letters.

With her husband still in Italy, Manny's sister, Mara, and her fiancé, Ricardo, would be there to greet her and take her back to the family home. It was truly a journey into the unknown. Would Manny's family accept her? What about his parents and their reaction to their new unknown daughter-in-law? How would she cope with being so far from her homeland? Dare she wonder whether she would ever get to see home again?

How could she even have such foolish thoughts? Rose questioned. She was exactly where she had always dreamed of being. America was not just a map now, brought out and pored over. It was actuality. This was where she was going to live. Although it was thousands of miles away, everything was a utopia. After years of devastation, hunger, and rationing, the many lights and abundance of food in the markets were unbelievable. Rose would quickly gorge herself with her eyes and stomach. She learned to eat hamburgers, hot dogs, steaks, and banana splits although her vanity had forbidden her in the past.

With Rose holding a small suitcase and a handbag, with her trunk at her side, Mara Catalano knew right away this was her new sister-in-law. Aside from seeing her name on the trunk, there was something cynical about her that prompted Mara to dislike her as soon as they introduced each other. This strange woman was her brother's choice of a life mate? This meant she was now her family too.

We don't have to be best friends, Mara considered, *but I guess I will be gracious and civil.* She realized if she didn't give Rose a chance, who knew what a turbulent road their family would encounter?

As soon as Rose got into the beautiful silver Pontiac Streamliner, she knew her life would be that of opulence and abundance. Her husband's family was drenched in wealth, and marrying Manny fulfilled all her dreams. He was of Italian descent, American, and most of all, rich. She was going to have the perfect life.

The drive to the Catalano Residence was only forty minutes, but to Rose, it seemed like hours. Not much was uttered between the new sisters-in-law. Rose, however, was intrigued with Ricardo and his consideration toward her, much to the obvious disapproval from Mara.

Rose noticed how attentive Ricardo was instantly but also observed Mara's dislike for her just as quickly.

I don't care if they like me or not, Rose concluded. In her own egotistical mind, she passed it off as pure jealousy. She and Manny were already married, so there was nothing anyone could do. Yet Rose questioned how it could possibly be for Mara to be jealous of a destitute foreigner from Italy when Mara herself was beautiful, swanky, and especially rich.

As they approached the Brooklyn Heights area, where she would be living, Rose was fascinated with the tree-lined blocks of classically inspired townhomes. When they finally pulled up to the beautiful Henry Street brownstone, her eyes were dazzled with excitement.

This is my home. She smiled as she got out of the vehicle. Taking in a gasp of air, she closed her eyes and reopened them to make sure she wasn't dreaming.

Brooklyn Heights was a posh residential area of elegant brownstones and was known for its promenade along the East River. It had outstanding views of Manhattan and the Statue of Liberty. It was a fascinating and exclusive neighborhood, with blocks of classically inspired mansions, picturesque streets, and plenty of greenery.

Rose was breathless when she entered the stunning, stately five-story, six-bedroom brownstone. It had a rear garden, exquisite details, and a rich storied past. While the housemaid, Gabrielle, directed Rose down the hallway, Mara and Ricardo went up the staircase instead of escorting her. Standing in the parlor were Manny's parents awaiting her arrival.

"Welcome," said the gentleman gazing at her. "I'm Giancarlo. This is my wife, Giorgia." After exchanging the cheek kiss, Rose noticed a stark glare on Giorgia's face. Not even a smile. Were these the people she would have to live with until her husband returned? She was afraid.

Giancarlo was exactly the type of man Rose had envisioned, only much better looking. She couldn't believe how handsome he was. He was suave, sophisticated, yet tenacious. Giorgia was beautiful and elegant like an Ava Gardner type—chic, classy, and graceful. Rose was becoming more and more intimidated as the day passed.

Gabrielle, the housemaid, had come in to whisper something in Giorgia's ear. After excusing herself, Giancarlo began questioning Rose about life back in Italy. She knew it was Mara who had summoned Giorgia to leave the room. She also noticed that mother and daughter began discussing *her*. Even though to them, she was probably nothing more than a gold-digging, penniless peasant, she would one day prove just how much they miscalculated her.

Rose was determined to confirm her place with the Catalano family and social circle. Aside from being vain and conceited, Rose was strong-willed. There was no way she was going to let her past dictate their judgment. She would spend the next few weeks mostly in her bedroom, researching the practices of the elite in New York. Their style of dress, mannerisms, and charm were what Rose made sure she would perfect.

Rose's determination outweighed her desolation while living in Brooklyn without her husband. The only person who seemed to take any mercy on her during these days was Gabrielle. She was an African American woman who had worked many years for the Catalanos. Unlike many of her friends who were also housemaids, Gabrielle had enormous respect for the family she worked for. When most maids were treated as subhuman, were badly paid, and lived in squalor, Gabrielle was never treated like the underclass. The Catalanos treated her like she was part of the family.

Listening to Gabrielle speak so highly and affectionately about her employers annoyed Rose. How could they be so rude and pompous with her yet be so considerate of the housemaid? Even Gabrielle's living quarters were superior to hers. Rose vowed she would not be second fiddle to a housemaid.

Wait until Manny gets home. They'll be sorry. She sneered.

A few nights later, the family sat around the dinner table together for the first time since Rose's arrival. A few of the Catalano friends were also present alongside Giancarlo, Giorgia, Mara, and Ricardo. Rose was introduced to Salvatore and his wife, Lucia; Giacomo and his wife, Nella; and Eduardo. No one paid much attention to Rose, but for once in her life, she didn't mind at all. She wanted to just take everyone and everything in as much as she could.

As she sat listening to them converse about business, she had learned all the men at the table worked for her father-in-law. Giancarlo was referred to as the *boss* or *chief*; Salvatore was *Commander;* Ricardo and Eduardo were captains, and Giacomo was their legal counsel. Rose couldn't understand how any of these men could possibly have any idea about the garment industry or fashion. Judging from their crude vocabulary, they didn't seem like the sophisticated types Giancarlo would associate himself with.

These men were big, vulgar, and vigorous. Their wives were not nearly as chic or as elegant as Giorgia. They were more boisterous, flashy, and excessive in their mannerisms. Considering their husbands were in the garment industry, even their fashion choices seemed tacky and tasteless. Something seemed off for Rose. These people were nothing compared to what she imagined when her husband explained his family's business. Fashion didn't even come up during their discussions.

Rose noticed their apprehension in continuing certain dialogue as they would look at her and then at one another. It was obvious they did not want her to know much, which she found offensive. But in time, she thought, they would come to welcome and trust her since she was part of the family now.

What are these people hiding? she wondered. If only Manny were there, she could inquire further, yet she would not ask any questions at this time.

After dinner, they collectively arose from the table and headed into the parlor, leaving Rose all by herself. Her eyes began to fill with tears. Barely did Rose ever cry, let alone get emotional around people.

But this was different. She felt like an outcast. Back in Italy, she was in such control and was influential. Here no one gave her any scrutiny. No one seemed to care.

Rose's sadness quickly turned to anger.

"I will go to my room now," Rose muttered to Gabrielle as she was clearing the table.

"Don't worry, dear. It will get better. They just need to get used to a new addition to their circle," Gabrielle reassured her. But the consolation did not comfort Rose's emotions. She decided that the next day, she would get out and familiarize herself with the area.

Rose was not only determined to turn herself into a legitimate American socialite but also needed to *study* everything she could about her new family so she could fit in. There was no way she would allow any of them to continue to view her as an underprivileged pauper. Tomorrow, she would put on her best clothes and fix herself up to look and feel exceptional, she affirmed herself.

The next morning, Rose began her walking expedition of the neighborhood. As she walked south on Henry street; she came upon the bustling Montague Street, which was a hotbed of shops, cafes and restaurants. This was truly a fascinating town, she reckoned.

For the first time since her arrival, Rose felt inspired and thankful. Brooklyn Heights was a sedate, leafy, and gorgeous array of churches, townhomes, and buildings. It had become home to many writers and artists, and Rose was completely captivated by the variety of architectural styles. She noticed kids playing in the strangely car-free streets, women cleaning off stoops while minding their babies and toddlers, neighbors chatting at their front doors, laundry hanging between buildings, and teenagers hanging around corner candy stores and newsstands.

Rose couldn't help but smile as she walked along the streets. She even stopped for an espresso at a nearby café to rest. There was a permanent smile on her face as she walked until she reached Furman Street. It was there she noticed destruction and rubble once again—only this time it was not due to war. Construction had begun along the waterfront for a new expressway.

Brooklyn Heights' wreckage was from development. The city's planner Robert Moses had declared much of Brooklyn Heights a slum area. He proposed to obliterate it by laying his new Brooklyn-Queens expressway straight through the middle of it. The project required the destruction of many row houses and historic residential buildings.

As Rose stood witnessing the demolition of many structures, her mind immediately went back to Italy. It seemed like a lifetime ago that she had not been there, but the thought of it made her tremble. Her view from where she was standing, however, was spectacular. It was a breathtaking panoramic take of the Lower Manhattan skyline.

Rose quickly reminded herself of how she ended up there. If she had not been in Italy, she would have never met Manny, hence why she was in America. After savoring a few moments of quiet, Rose started heading back home. She concluded that even though the family wouldn't take notice, it was getting dark, and it was time to go back.

When she reached the residence, Rose settled on the stoop for a while before going inside. While pondering where her life was heading, Rose couldn't help but feel uneasy about the members of her new household. Manny seemed so different from the rest of them. Was he, or was it just the uniform that was the contrast? Maybe he would be like them once he was home in his own element.

It felt so long since Rose had seen Manny. Her loneliness was becoming intolerable. Even though she did not miss her homeland, this new land wasn't as amicable as she had envisioned. What was more disappointing was the unfavorable reception by his family. Rose and Manny did not have a traditional wedding back in Italy. However, she had hoped that once they were in America, they would be given some sort of soirée. Given the way the family was conducting themselves, she realized that a dazzling reception in their honor would probably never take place.

When Rose entered the house and began to walk up the many stairs to her fifth-level bedroom, she stumbled upon Giancarlo and a few of his friends. His study, located on the third level of their brownstone, was a beautiful room of paneled walls and high ceilings. A fire burned in the fireplace, casting a warm glow over the area where he and his companions sat, relaxed and sipping Courvoisier cognac. Her perception of the meeting was of course business, but her curiosity had her deliberating whether it was about garments and fashion or *other* matters.

Instead of heading into her bedroom, Rose decided to tip-toe back down a few stairs so she could hear the conversation. She quickly became stunned and alarmed by what she was hearing. The conversation seemed to have nothing to do with business but rather a debate about a showdown. Giancarlo intervened and took over the discussion.

"I need you to set up a meeting between Frank, Willie, and myself," Rose overheard Giancarlo ask one of his *friends*. He continued, "Now that Lucky is out of the picture, it will be easier to set up. Frank's a good guy, and I know he'll hear us out."

"Come on, *Cat*. We have a past with this person, which isn't a very good one. I don't like the Lucianos getting involved in our affairs," affirmed one of the other voices.

"Eddy, we're small fish in a huge fuckin' pond now. La Camorra is dying, and the Sicilians are takin' over. We either jump on board or sink and drown." *Eddy*, that name Rose knew. He was the handsome single playboy she had met at dinner one night.

Rose observed the other voice responding to Eddy sounded like Ricardo, Mara's fiancé. She had noticed them as she passed the study, but there were some other faces she had never seen before. What she couldn't figure out was why they referred to her father-in-law as *Cat*.

While continuing to hear what they were discussing, she became startled by Giancarlo's stern and resilient stance. Rose was intrigued by her father-in-law. He was dapper, dashing, and stylish in his well-tailored clothes. She was witnessing a volatile side to him that she found very gripping.

"Frank will need to pass all this by Lucky, but Vito will go for it for sure. For one, Vito is a *paisane*, and two, the fashion house makes lots of cash. It's a lucrative business, and they'll definitely want pieces of the pie."

"Exactly," shouted Eddy, "so why do we need to give these bums anything when we've been doin' so good on our own?" Ricky intervened.

"Because we're losing respect and control of the neighborhood! Not to mention, we don't have the pull like we used to with the feds, politicians, and other people we need. If we join the Sicilians, we'll have these guys in our pockets, make far more money, and have anything we want at our disposal."

"Ricky! Eddy! Shut the fuck up, both of you!" Giancarlo demanded. "Just set this meetin' up, and let's get it done! I don't want debates about nothin', ya hear?"

When Rose quietly began walking down a few more steps, a voice inquired, "Rose, what are you doing?" It was Gabrielle walking up the flight of stairs. Rose was startled and couldn't even answer.

Giancarlo knew right away that Rose had been listening to their conversation. He could tell she was curious by the look on her face when she passed by, but he didn't think she was that much of a *nosy broad*. Looking over at Giancarlo, Eddy hinted quietly, "Cat, what the fuck? You think she heard us?"

"Don't worry about my daughter-in-law. She barely understands English, but I'll make sure she understands never to meddle in the family business."

Rose knew that Gabrielle catching her eavesdropping on Giancarlo was not going to go over well. She quickly went up into her bed and hid under the covers like she had just seen a ghost. Rose immediately realized she was acting cowardly and childishly.

Even though she didn't sleep much that night, the next morning, Rose awakened early enough to get out of the house before everyone was up for breakfast. Her inquisitive nature led her to go into the town again to get information on her new family. What did the feds and politicians have to do with fashion? she wondered. Why were the men in that study referring to her father-in-law as *Cat*? At one point, she remembered hearing someone being referred to as Spitz.

The next few days, Rose spent her time investigating. She would read newspapers and magazines and even started to ask many in the community questions about the Catalanos. These were questions that one of her father-in-law's associates would soon discover and report back to Giancarlo. When he heard this news, he became furious. He instantly sent a telegram to his son, Manny, and ordered him to return home urgently.

In the telegram, Giancarlo made Manny believe it was an emergency. His son was to return at once, but he made no mention of why. This panicked Manny. He didn't know what to do. He understood that when his father demanded something, there was no way of refusing him.

The thought of leaving Naples and never seeing Lilly again was torturous. Although she was married to Luca and he was married to Rose, he knew that somehow their odyssey was not over. There was no way he would allow it to be. He vowed that their journey would continue one day, even if it was months or years from that moment.

Rose was used to corruption, black market activities, and *La Camorra*, the Neapolitan Mafia-type crime syndicate. Growing up in and around Naples, her recognition of this enterprise was more than competent, especially during the war years. She was completely astounded by the knowledge that her new family engaged in similar exercises.

In just a few days, Rose had discovered they were a minor force of the New York–based Camorra. The fight over the control of the New York rackets between La Camorra and the Sicilian Mafia had started in the early part of the century, leading La Camorra to dwindle over the last few years. Giancarlo was the actual *capo* of his gang of Camorristi, but he had come to realize his declining power and diminishing wealth was due to the rise of *La Cosa Nostra*.

After overhearing the conversation between her father-in-law and his crew a few days earlier and doing some research of her own, Rose concluded that the Catalano organization wanted to merge with the bigger players of the syndicate.

Since the Catalanos owned a lucrative garment and fashion house, revenue was good, especially at the beginning of the war, when they began to specialize in war uniforms and attire. However, since the war was over, it was time to join higher ranks and make more money.

This newfound knowledge about the family enticed Rose to a new level of elation. The discovery was arousing and stimulating, and she found herself completely enthralled by her father-in-law and his *friends*. In America, mobsters were like celebrities who cared about their communities and lived by their codes of honor and conduct.

In Italy, she found gangsters vulgar, bestial, and unpolished. American mobsters seemed more sophisticated, classy, and refined. They completely turned her on. She wondered if Manny was just as deeply involved as his father, or if he was the black sheep of the family. It was evident to her that Mara played a major role in her father's organization, especially her fiancé, Ricky. But Manny had never spoken of these activities to her while he was in Italy.

Rose couldn't wait any longer for Manny to return. She had so many questions, and she was tired of the solitude. Her mind was always racing. She didn't dare ask her in-laws about their enterprise; however, with Manny by her side, perhaps they could be somehow be integrated into the mix.

Imagine having all that power and money, she wondered. She could hardly control her growing excitement as the day of Manny's arrival came closer.

"Your husband will be arriving tomorrow, my dear," a voice said behind her. While Rose was walking up to her bedroom quarters, she turned.

"Gabrielle, you startled me."

"I'm sorry, my dear Rose. I just wanted to give you the good news since no one else around here would," she said as she winked. Gabrielle liked Rose even though she knew the family didn't feel the same. Gabrielle could tell Rose was an indifferent prima donna, but there was a softness and sadness in this passionate flower's eyes. No one could see it, but Gabrielle could, and she was always more sympathetic and sensitive of her.

Rose was angry that no one had informed her of Manny's arrival at first. How could they not let her know? She was his wife whether they liked it or not.

I'll show them! She grunted. Although she had things going against her, she would forge ahead despite all that. One day, she would prove to her new family and the rest of the world that she was not just some peasant war bride. Rose would not settle for being just a traditional wife who cooked, cleaned, and raised children either.

The next morning, as she awakened, Rose could hear voices and laughter coming from the lower levels. It was when she heard Giorgia and Mara crying of joy when she realized Manny had arrived.

"Oh dio!" she fretted. What would they think of her still in bed and not ready to welcome her husband home? As Rose stumbled to get ready, she turned to find Manny already in the doorway.

"Rosanna, how are you?"

"I'm sorry, Manuele. I wasn't informed of your arrival earlier," she snarled.

"I just asked how you are, Rosie," he asserted.

Rose was livid. Firstly, his family had not informed her of her husband's arrival sooner, and secondly, Manny hadn't greeted her with any sentiment or warmth. There was a coldness about him that was disturbing and troublesome.

Is this how their marriage was going to be? she worried. Quickly she recognized she was now in the land of opportunity, and no one, not even her husband, would hamper her ambitions. She would never be submissive to the will of anyone but her own.

Rose could tell Manny was preoccupied as he unpacked all his belongings. The conversation was brief, and he specified he was tired and wanted to sleep. She decided to go out and relish the streets once again. Now that her husband was finally home, she could start preparing for her future—a future that she vowed would consist of plenty of wealth, power, and prestige.

While roaming the streets, Rose contemplated different ideas as to how to make herself an asset to the Catalano family. After several weeks of observations and paying attention to their practices, she knew exactly what was required to make an impact. She needed to make them more money. As she sat down for an espresso at a local café, she planned her strategy. She was very knowledgeable when it came to the black market and the Camorra.

The days and weeks passed, and Rose was finally accepting of her new home. It was now December, and the Thanksgiving feast and celebrations were over. This would be her first Christmas in America. New York was beautiful in the winter. She had never experienced real white snow. The only snow she had ever seen was the gray ashes falling from the eruption of Mount Vesuvius or the remnants of war. She had never witnessed anything so beautiful and began to take the ferry across to Manhattan often. Taking long strolls in Central Park, she had never walked so much in her life. She was taking in the crisp, fresh air, festive decorations, and most of all, the fine shops of Fifth Avenue.

Rose's desire for opulence and exuberance had become an obsession. Her excessive greed and hunger for money was always evident from when she was a little girl. Being in the United States, she had so many opportunities at her doorstep—from her in-laws' fashion business and lavish lifestyle to all the aristocrats that surrounded her. Rose was determined more than ever to become the chic, elegant socialite she felt she was meant to be. Her determination to become more prominent had became an unreasonable obsession.

Rose came up with an idea, one that would make her an abundance of cash but haunt her in the future. After witnessing many years of corruption, bribery, and prostitution in Italy, she learned that those profiting were not poor citizens but the Camorra or high-ranking officers.

Although forms of entertainment seemed to capture the attention of servicemen in Naples during the war, Rose undoubtedly knew that prostitution was very lucrative. Since the Catalanos were already wealthy, she believed she would have access to immense funds. However, not only did she not obtain any affection; her in-laws would only provide her with the necessities. This made her crave prestige, status, and power even more than wealth.

Over the next few weeks, she used her looks, sexuality, and negotiating skills in recruiting underage girls for prostitution. Just like her mother, Dahlia, she would enlist in the advantageous trade. Rose then set up a meeting with Ricardo and Eduardo to discuss the benefits of their participation. She would give them full recognition and very profitable revenue. Her participation, however, would be kept in silence from her in-laws and husband. She would negotiate part control of the enterprise but full domination of the girls.

Bringing Ricardo into the mix was a very risky move, considering he was Mara's fiancé. But his hunger for wealth and money guaranteed his cooperation and silence. Eduardo, being the ever-handsome but tough playboy of the bunch, would be completely on board with this endeavor.

Ricardo was turned on by this intriguing woman from Naples. Listening to her arbitrate this venture was very captivating. Rose herself could sense the sexual attraction between her and her soon-to-be brother in-law. Although Eddy was the good-looking model type, Ricky was much more masculine and vigorous, which aroused her in a raw, animalistic way.

Rose was on a mission to find the most vulnerable and poorest of young girls. With her persuasion, she was able to achieve her objective. Manny would be oblivious to his wife's activities, spending most of his time thinking about Lili. He couldn't get her out of his mind. Although Manny wasn't working yet, he wanted nothing to do with the family business, either the garment industry or the extracurricular activities his father was involved in.

Giancarlo and Giorgia realized the day their son arrived that Manny was not happy with his marriage to this audacious, cold Italian girl from Naples. Although Manny didn't want to follow in his father's footsteps, Giancarlo always had an extraordinary affection for his only son, as did his mother, Giorgia. Mara was closer to her mother than father, but she was always the more detached and irresponsible child of the two. This made both parents idolize their son much more than their daughter.

CHAPTER SIX

"What's wrong, my love?" Luca consoled his wife after seeing her lying on their bed all morning.

"I will be fine. I'm just tired from all the work that we have been doing to this house. I just need some rest," Lili stressed. She was not feeling well for the last few days but pushed forward so her husband wouldn't worry. Contemplating, she realized maybe it was time she saw a doctor.

In the last three months since moving to Benevento, Lili felt really drained. However, she had finally found serenity. Life was good now. She had not gone to see her parents' grave sites for a while and thought it was time. Since she was going to go see them, she would also go and visit Dottore Vittorio Conte.

Lili didn't really want to go back to Portici. It had too many atrocious memories. Nonetheless, it was her hometown, and she would go only to see the doctor. She trusted Dottore Conte like her mother did and knew he would take good care of her. As she thought about what she knew about her mother, anxiety quickly set in. How would she face the townsfolk should they see her? What would they say to her? What would she say to them? After all, she and Luca did disappear, and everyone in the town was probably aware of her mother's past.

Lili spent most of her time in bed or in the lavatory, vomiting. After a few days, she and Luca finally took the drive to Portici. They would go to the doctor's first and then visit the grave sites on the way home. As they entered the town, it still looked as gloomy and depressing as she remembered. Not much of the rubble and debris had been cleaned up, and the people looked just as distraught as they did the day she and Luca left. Lili did notice the changes in demeanors. As they walked to the doctor's home, the insults began, just as Dottore Conte had predicted.

People standing in doorways or along the street or walking by began calling her names like *puttana* and whore. At first, she thought it was because of her mother's trade in the past two years. She then discovered the remarks were directed at her for marrying her sister's ex-beau.

What disgusting hypocrisy this was, she thought to herself. The same people who used to admire her were the very people who were judging her mother and *her*. How dare these bigots criticize her and her family? Most of them participated in black market activities to survive, and many of the women had turned to prostitution also. It was no secret.

Still, how did she not ever realize what her own mother was doing? So many women turned to sex to make money, but her mother? How was her marriage to her sister's ex-beau a higher level of immorality than what most Neapolitans were guilty of? Lili was consumed by all these baffling thoughts.

As she began to cry, Dr. Conte opened his door.

"Come in, my dear," he said quietly. "Please, into my salotto." He continued, "It is nice to see you again, my dear. As you can see, nothing has changed. The people are worse." He could see the anguish in Lili's eyes but reassured her that she and Luca made the right decision to move away.

"I'm not feeling very well, Dottore. I've been very tired, and my stomach is always hurting." She sighed.

"What do you mean, your stomach has been hurting? How?" Lili didn't answer, so after a long pause, he added, "I suggest you and

I go into the other room while Luca waits here. I will need to examine you." He did examine her but without an internal.

The doctor knew right away what Lili's discomfort was from. Luca sat patiently when they entered back into the *salotto*. Luca couldn't help but notice how white and pale Lili's face was. It wasn't her usual angelic appearance but a ghastly zombie look.

As she walked toward Luca, Lili collapsed.

"Oh dio!!" Luca screamed. "Dottore Conte! What is happening?"

The doctor paused for a moment and then declared, "Lilianna is pregnant." A baby? Luca started to tremble. He couldn't believe what he was hearing. How was this possible? He could not ejaculate with his condition, so the sex was never *completed*. He could feel his heart racing, and he began to have shortness of breath. As his wife began to regain consciousness after fainting, he, too, felt like he was going to slump to the floor.

Luca knew exactly why Lili fainted. She was probably just as shocked as he was. Their reactions were not due to being overjoyed but too much distress. Lili and Luca both knew he was not the father of this baby. It was impossible. Even the dottore knew. He was the only doctor in town and was fully aware of Luca's condition. How would they continue now with this lie?

Driving home, Lili and Luca did not speak a word to each other. When they stopped by the cemetery, Lili cried profusely at her parents' grave sites. Luca wandered around in a daze, just reading the headstones of others. He couldn't console his wife at all. They did not mutter one word to each other. When he began walking back to his vehicle, Lili noticed. Then she, too, walked toward the truck and got in without uttering a word.

Lili and Luca headed back to Benevento. Once they arrived home, she went directly into the bedroom while he went to sit at the kitchen table. Lili knew this was Manny's child. Luca was bewildered. His mind was racing with a million thoughts. Who could the father possibly be? He had already discovered Lili was not a virgin on their wedding night. As soon as he noticed there were no bloodstains from their lovemaking, he knew she had had sex with someone else. But now she was carrying his child!

Luca was completely broken. For the next couple of days, he and Lili did not speak to each other. Lili stayed at home, resting and contemplating what to do next. Luca would take off in his truck for hours. She didn't know exactly where he would go, and she dared not ask. They had only been married a mere three months, and already their marriage was in turmoil.

I wonder what Manny and Rose are doing, Lili pondered. As she lay on her bed, she began to shed tears. The thought of him sharing the same bed with her despicable sister made her nauseous even more. Rose was free of all this agony. She was living in America, living a great life away from the dread of Italy. The vain and pretentious Rose had been given the golden opportunity. This annoyed and debilitated Lili. How did this all happen?

Lili had decided to take a walk in the fields around her home. It was a beautiful day, and lying in bed, wallowing in her sorrows, would only intensify her fragility. She had a baby to think about now, and this baby was her world—not Luca, not Manny, not anyone. Her child was her only new focus and nothing else.

When she returned home, Luca pulled up in his truck. To her surprise, he had gone into town and brought back some fresh vegetables from a friend's garden.

"Come, Lili, I will make the dinner tonight. I know you still do not feel well." Lili was delightfully amazed. What was with his change of heart?

When they sat to eat their dinner, Luca began speaking to Lili as if nothing had ever happened. Luca never made any reference to the pregnancy, only speaking about the people in Benevento and their neighbors. He filled her in on all the new gossip circulating as a way of reassuring her they were not the only ones subjected to turmoil. They once again carried on as before.

The baby's development and Lili's stomach began to grow; the two of them still would not discuss the issue. The only references made toward the pregnancy were when the townsfolk would inquire.

Luca and Lili referred to the baby as *their* child. No one was aware of Luca's shortcomings. Therefore, it was in their best interest that everyone believed this was *his* baby.

Remembering her mother's past, Lili couldn't help but compare her situation to Dahlia's. Like her mother, she too was expecting the child of another man that was not her husband. Now she understood her mother's heartache, carrying the child of a man who was the love of your life yet who was married to another.

While her baby grew, Lili's ailments became more about heartache than physical aches. She had a good husband, a baby on the way, and a new home. But she had never felt so isolated. She missed her mother and father immensely, and nothing or no one could ever bring them back. It was a void that would never be filled again.

The thought of her mother selling herself was another factor Lili couldn't comprehend. Although prostitution had become a common circumstance during the war; she would never have imagined her own mother capable of having sex with random men. Yet she still loved and adored Dahlia deeply despite her sins. Lili had committed many sins of her own. She understood hardships and heartaches, and for this, she forgave her.

Luca, however, was not as forgiving with Lili. Although they functioned as a married couple on the outside, he no longer shared the same bed with Lili. Knowing his wife was carrying another man's baby was agonizing. Although for a while they tried, his pride couldn't continue to comply with the charade in private.

Going through a devastating war was already enough. Now, with all this added chaos, it was getting to be more than Luca could handle. Why was God being so harsh to them? he glumly thought to himself.

"I will go to sleep now," Lili sadly said to Luca as he sat at the kitchen table.

"Good night. I will go into town early morning. Do you need anything in particular?" he asked.

"No. I think I have everything I need." Lili stared at him dejectedly. He was no longer the same man after all these months. But who could blame him? she reflected. Neither of them would ever be the same again.

When Lili walked away, Luca's head felt like it was spinning. The more he examined the circumstances, the more he became outraged.

Maybe she is just like her sister, he began to determine angrily. *That angelic face is just a sham. She, her sister, and her mother, the whore—they're all whores!* Luca slammed the teacup to the floor shattering in a thousand pieces.

Lili heard the clamor but did not go and see. She had already guessed at his fury, and it was hard for her to fall asleep. Feeling agitated and uncomfortable, she decided to get up and inspect the "sacred" storage box her mother had asked her to forever hold on to. As Lili brought it back to her bed and sat down, she hesitated for a few minutes before opening it. She hadn't checked what was in it yet.

Anxiously lifting the lid of the somewhat small treasure trunk, Lili wasn't sure of what to expect other than Dahlia's valuables. The first item she saw was a Franciscan wooden rosary. As Lili began to shuffle through, she also came across a medal chain of St. Anthony of Padua and a filigree ring of the Madonna, Mother Mary. Underneath these cherished items were a pile of documents and letters. She carefully took them out and began reading them one by one.

The first document was a copy of her parents' marriage certificate. It was dated April 1930. She was born October 1929. Lili became disoriented. How was this possible? She was born *before* her parents married? Having a child out of wedlock was already scandalous. Dahlia having had Rose so many years earlier was disreputable, but her too? Oh dio! She couldn't imagine the devastation and turmoil her mother must have endured.

Lili had even worn Dahlia's wedding dress when she and Luca married, the very dress her mother had hand sewn herself. It was a beautiful vintage 1920s-inspired dress that would have long been out of style by 1930.

The next document was Lili's birth certificate. Her heart began to pound rapidly. The name of her mother was stated; however, where it indicated "father," it stated "unknown."

Unknown? Lili felt faintness and dizziness when a sense of terror came over her. She had already learned about an illicit affair her mother had had with a wealthy married man. Could she also be the spawn of someone else, or did Dahlia and Paolo just commit a major sin before marriage?

Lili had to get answers. She wouldn't rest until she knew the whole story. How did Dahlia care for Rose if her father and mother were not married until 1930? Rose was nine years old when Lili was born. She decided to send her sister a letter. Not feeling well due to her pregnancy, the letter took her a couple of days to write. But she made sure to make it clear that her sister give her as much information as she could.

Lili had no doubt Rose knew something, given how she was never the loving sibling. There were reasons behind her sister's displeasure of her. Lili was learning more and more regarding the circumstances surrounding Rose's childhood. All this was explaining Rose's bitterness and jealousy toward her and her callousness toward her parents.

Rose always felt like she was the black sheep of the family, and Lili was considered the golden child. To Rose, everything she would say or do was always marginalized. Whereas with Lili, everything was praised and valued. They were always compared not only by their parents but also by everyone around them.

In her letter, Lili would just get straight to the point.

Rosanna,

> I hope all is well. My purpose for this letter is not to interrupt your prosperity and happiness. However, I feel that it is your responsible duty, as my sister, to be as honest as possible. Please tell me the truth about our childhood. Rosanna, I know you were just a child when our mother and father married. But you were old enough to understand, so I am positive that you were aware

of this matter. I ask that you at least give me some clarification as to how the events in our lives unfolded. Please, Rose, tell me what you know.

Lilianna

As Lili sealed the envelope, a sudden surge of anxiety came over her. Just the thought of Rose with Manny made her heart rate accelerate. Who knew if her sister would even respond to the letter? However, no matter what happened, Lili had something Rose didn't—Manny's child. Or did she? What if Rose also got pregnant? The palpitations began to increase until Lili comforted herself in believing her sister was far too vain to let her body deform from carrying a child. Her goal in going to America had nothing to do with family. It had to do with wealth and fortune.

The weeks were passing by, and her baby was growing. Luca wouldn't speak much with Lili, but they carried on in public, like any other couple awaiting the birth of their child. Still, the child was *not* Luca's, and they both knew that.

All Lili could think of was Manny. What was he doing? What was he thinking? Was he even happy with Rose? So many questions and not enough answers. Lili was overwhelmed with all the uncertainty. There was so much ambiguity surrounding her life and her family's past. Everything was so confusing.

For the first time in a long time, Lili started to experience intense fear. It was a despair like she experienced during the war. Although the war was over, these conflicts were different. They were new battles to fight. That's when Lili realized that life was a battlefield of all kinds of wars. It was up to her to either fight and conquer or surrender.

In the last few days, Lili was feeling uncomfortable not only mentally but also physically. She was experiencing abdominal pain and cramps, nausea, and dizziness. Was this due to her pregnancy or stress? she wondered. Lili was now in her thirty-sixth week and knew it was still early.

That night she couldn't sleep. Her mind and body were drained. The pain had gotten unbearable, so she decided to wake her husband.

"Luca, I am not feeling well. I think we must go."

"Where do you want to go at this hour?" Luca answered Lili, quite annoyed. She presumed he was still half-asleep and had not yet realized what she was asking him.

"Luca! The baby!" she asserted but then bent over in extreme pain, and noticed herself bleeding. When Luca got out of bed, he noticed the blood and his wife in agony.

"Liliana! Oh dio mio! We must go to the hospital now!"

"Yes, I know!" she muttered and then began crying.

Lili began screaming when the pain got more intense. Luca put a towel between his wife's legs as her bleeding was becoming more excessive. After managing to get into the vehicle, Luca began accelerating. Not only was Lili in pain, but she was also terrified.

The drive to the hospital took only ten minutes. When they entered the medical facility, several nurses rushed to Lili's side after noticing the amount of blood she had lost. They immediately brought her to a room. By the time the doctor came in, Lili's cervix was at six centimeters. Because she was still so young, many girls of Lili's age were not fully grown, so their pelvises were not ready for childbirth, causing an increased risk of complications.

The doctors and nurses realized they had to perform an emergency C-section to get the baby out as soon as possible. Seconds after delivering her baby, Lili's vital signs stopped for about twenty-five seconds. She was diagnosed with an amniotic fluid embolism, a rare condition that occurred when amniotic fluid or fetal material entered the mother's bloodstream and could cause death.

Lili had died for a few moments. Luca was frantic and filled with despair. He couldn't believe what was happening. He had no one, and now that he had Lili, even she would be taken away. However, he would be left with a brand-new baby boy, the son of his nemesis.

Luca had known for a long time that Manny was the one who had impregnated Lili. From the first time he recognized him at Lili's apartment; he sensed something cynical. Now, he would be responsible for a child who belonged to another man—the man who held captive the hearts of the two women Luca had ever loved.

Despite being in a coma for a few days and spending several weeks in the hospital, Lili beat the odds and survived. They still had not given the baby a name, but Lili had no doubt in her mind she would name her son after her father. She would call him Gian-Paolo. But what about his last name? What would they put on the birth certificate? Would Luca allow her son to carry his name even though he was not his?

After much deliberation, Luca decided he would give the child his name. After all, what would people say when he was growing up and had a different last name from his? To show face, Luca did the respectable thing. However, the boy would also take on his mother's name, Gian-Paolo Bianchi Marchese.

CHAPTER SEVEN

With Ricky and Eddy on board, Rose's vision of her new lucrative enterprise became more apparent now. The two men had turned an old run-down bar into a new "social club" where men could meet, mingle, and engage in extracurricular activities. There was an array of many beautiful young girls who would entertain them in one of the rooms situated upstairs.

The bar was situated in Newark, New Jersey, far enough from Brooklyn Heights, where people in their social circle would never frequent. Even *the Boss*, Giancarlo, would never go there. He was a New Yorker, and he would never be seen in what he felt was a seedy place like Newark.

Rose's job was to select the girls and make sure they were properly prepared and groomed for their appointments. She would frequent the garment factory to pick up sexy lingerie and undergarments for the girls. The employees dared not ask her any questions as most of them just thought they were for her. Ricky and Eddy were responsible for the other employees of the bar. They were also the "muscle" in case any of the clients would get out of line.

The flow of cash seemed to be endless. Rose had picked up so many beautiful, young, yet poor and vulnerable girls. Although they were impoverished and destitute, they were quickly reformed and coached by Rose. They were made to look and feel like higher-class hookers instead of meager and desperate prostitutes.

Rose had twelve girls at the onset, but soon the number of girls grew. The more girls they had working, the more money they had coming in. Many men became regulars. Rose kept a log of everything, making sure all the money was accounted for. The club was coincidentally called Broad Street Gentlemen's Club, located on Broad Street in a seedy area of Newark.

Ricky and Eddy would be there every night. They still worked for the Catalano clan, yet Giancarlo looked more to his consigliere Giacomo "Jack" Moretti and commander underboss Sammy "Spitz" Spinelli to look after all the *management of the business*. Although Ricardo would soon be his son-in-law, Giancarlo did not have much confidence in him. He saw Ricky as more of a sidekick wannabe instead of a true wiseguy for the family. Giancarlo was convinced the only reason Ricky started dating his daughter was so he could get into business with the Catalano clan.

Nonetheless, his daughter had fallen in love with him. Even if Ricardo was not exactly a worldly or refined man, he was loyal. Loyalty was the main attribute Giancarlo looked for in all his crew members. Soon, Ricardo would be family. So he let him do what he wanted most of the time. Ricky knew that when *the Boss* called or he was asked to do something, he would always oblige.

Mara, his loving fiancé, was noticing the extent of his absenteeism. Her beloved Ricky didn't seem to be around as often as before. But when she would question him, his usual response would be "But, babe, I keep thinking you are busy planning and doing girlie wedding stuff. You know that shit doesn't interest me. I trust you to make all the arrangements."

Mara was cognizant of her soon-to-be husband's allegiance to her father. Whatever Giancarlo wanted or needed, everyone had to kneel to his every wish. After all, he was the leader of the money train. Without Giancarlo and his business, no one would be *eating*. He was the capo of everyone and everything. She was far too used to the lifestyle her parents had created to ruffle any unnecessary feathers.

"Ms. Rosanna, there is a telegram I placed on your night table, next to your bed," Gabrielle cautioned Rose before she headed up the stairs to her room.

"Telegram? From who?" Rose blurted. She couldn't determine who it could possibly be. Her parents were dead, she didn't have any friends, and her sister would *never* send her a telegram.

When she entered her bedroom, Manny was already asleep. She opened it quickly and was dazed by the sender. It was *Lilith*. Why was she sending her this? Did Manny read it before her?

Although she was nervous, her anxiety quickly turned to anger after reading it.

How dare she send her this nonsense and ask silly questions about their family? As far as Rose was concerned, their history together had ended. She was in America, building a new life, and Lili was in Italy, living her own life. There was absolutely no reason to answer her.

As morning broke, Manny was getting dressed when he noticed his wife was waking up.

"Did you read the telegram?" he blatantly asked Rose.

"Yes, and I suppose you did too," she snarled.

"Yes, I did, so? I'm your husband. What is yours is mine," Manny retorted back. "What is that all about?"

Rose, trying to simplify the telegram, just jabbered, "My sister is overdramatic and probably has too much time on her hands, so she's delusional and immature."

Usually Manny would have been shocked by this response, but he had now been with Rose long enough to know she was a callous, heartless, and greedy dame. All she cared about was prestige and wealth. He knew she was up to something, but it didn't matter what Rose did. He simply didn't want to know and did not care anymore.

They had not had sex in weeks. He had reached a point where he no longer desired his wife anymore. All he could think of was Lili. The mere thought of touching and seeing her again made him weak at the knees. He believed in his heart and mind that day would come again.

As the weeks passed, Manny kept himself busy by doing lots of reading and visiting with friends. He would sometimes stop by the factory just to make sure everything was running smoothly. Although he wanted nothing to do with the business, it was the least he could do for his father since he did not have any other job. He also didn't want to disappoint Giancarlo, who constantly inquired about his son's activities. Giancarlo made sure Manny was kept busy and was doing something productive with his time.

Rose, however, was very active. She was never home and was always out and about. When Giorgia and Mara questioned Manny about his wife, he would simply tell them it was none of their business. The truth was he didn't care. The more she was out, the more at peace he felt. He did much thinking about his future and knew this road he had taken with Rose would not take him far.

"We did really good tonight, boys," beamed Rose in her broken English.

"Oh yeah?" Ricky marveled.

"Oh yeah, handsome, we are doing more and more every day."

"That's because you are a pretty good manager, doll." Rose giggled as she and Ricky exchanged long, seductive stares at each other.

Eddy noticed it right away. Feeling uncomfortable, he quickly said, "Okay, I'm outta here. I'm so friggin' tired."

Neither Rose nor Ricky answered him as he bolted down the stairs to get out of the bar.

Rose didn't usually stay at the bar at this late hour, but after having had a spat with Manny, she wanted to be away from the house as long as possible on this evening. She was a lonely woman who had been disregarded by everyone, especially her own husband. They hadn't had sex in a long time, and she was deprived of sexual gratification.

When she and Ricky realized they were alone, they decided to have some drinks together to celebrate the evening's success. As one drink led to another, they both became too intoxicated to go anywhere. One thing the alcohol did do was highly increase their sexual appetite. Before either one of them could stop each other, their clothes were off.

Ricky slipped two fingers inside her while his thumb rubbed around her sweet spot. He kept his mouth on her breasts, going from one to the other, sucking on her hardened nipples. Rose hadn't felt this kind of ecstasy in a long time. He put her on top of the table and spread her legs wide open. His thrusts were pumping into her hard and raw, just the way she loved it. When she yanked his hair to pull him closer, he drove his tongue inside her mouth to plunder hers.

Ricky ejaculated more quickly than Rose would have liked, but given the circumstances, it was probably a good thing they finished quickly. After noticing the time, Ricky offered to take Rose home immediately. Chances were no one would see him, but they had to get home before anyone would notice. Although he knew he probably shouldn't be driving, he took the chance.

When Rose arrived home, all the lights were out.

Oh dio, she fretted. Her husband was probably asleep, and he wouldn't care where she was anyway. He had made that quite clear in the last few weeks. It seemed that anything she did or said did not interest him in the least. At first, it pained her when she realized he had become so unattached, but since her new endeavor, it was probably a good thing.

One thing she wasn't counting on when she entered the home was Gabrielle, the curious and intrusive housemaid.

Why is this woman always in my face? Rose fumed.

"Was that Mr. Ricky in the car?" Gabrielle queried when Rose entered the house.

"Gabrielle, it was a long day. Good night."

Rose avoided the question, pretending not hear it, but Gabrielle knew full well she did. It was him! This had now ignited Gabrielle's curiosity to a new level. She never trusted Rose from the beginning. At first, it seemed that Gabrielle was the only one who had warmed to her. However, even Gabrielle had caught on to Rose's deviousness.

Manny heard his wife come into the room but pretended to sleep. Although he didn't care much for Rose these days, he was curious as to what she had been doing with her time this last little while. What was she doing on her own? he wondered. She wasn't exactly close to his family and clearly had no friends. She seemed to be buying many things but presumed she didn't have access to the amount with what she was purchasing. That's when he realized she was up to something.

The next morning, Rose slipped out as soon as she could to avoid seeing anyone, especially Gabrielle. But the clever housemaid was onto her and watching her every move.

"Good morning, Manny." She smiled as he was coming down the staircase. "Good morning, Gabby."

"Your wife slipped out quite early this morning. She's been keeping busy, I see," Gabrielle hinted.

"Yes, she needs to be productive, so that's good for her," Manny emphasized. It wasn't exactly the response Gabrielle was hoping for as she was considering telling him about her ride from Ricardo. But then she realized it was best that she didn't say anything *yet*.

In his study, Giancarlo was becoming more and more agitated. He quickly dialed the telephone.

"Sammy! What's going on with the meeting? Is it set up yet or what?"

"Well yeah, I've talked to them but nothin' confirmed yet."

"Jesus Christ!" Giancarlo fumed. "How long is this shit going to keep going on for? By the way, where the fuck those two clowns been lately?"

"Who? Ricky and Eddy?" Sammy guessed.

"Yeah, where the fuck they been?" Giancarlo ranted.

Lately Ricky and Eddy seemed to be too busy too often and were not coming around as usual. Everyone within *la famiglia* had noticed, and Giancarlo was furious.

"I want them both here tonight! We need to start getting our act together if we want to merge with the Sicilians. We're becoming too fuckin' sloppy and careless."

As Giancarlo slammed the phone, he noticed Gabrielle in the doorway.

"Gabby, what's up?" Gabrielle hesitated. She wanted to tell him she had seen Ricardo, his soon to be son-in-law, with his daughter-in-law but realized if she did, he would know she was listening in on his conversation.

I will let it go for now and save it for another time, she considered. "You look like you could use something, Mr. C. Is there anything I can getcha?"

"I'm good, Gabby. I don't need anything." He glared at her, wondering how much of the "business" she knew about over the years.

Giancarlo didn't like that Gabrielle might know so much, but she was loyal to his family, and they never had any issues with her. He knew he could trust her to a certain degree, but that didn't mean she needed to know every aspect of their lives. Gabrielle knew the consequences that would come with disloyalty, so she would never disclose anything to anyone.

Every Sunday afternoon, Gabrielle would meet with other housemaid friends for tea. She made them all believe she had the ideal job and worked for the best household. But most of the others knew exactly who she worked for. Everyone in Brooklyn Heights and most of New York City knew who the Catalanos were. If not for their extracurricular activities, they were known for their garment business.

The Catalanos always seemed to survive, even flourish in unexpected ways. Most of the elite from New York City's finest shopped at the Catalano Fashion House, especially when the war broke out. Since materials were rationed, most garment industries had limited resources. However, the Catalanos never seemed to be in short supply. It was their lucrative garment enterprise that got them the so-desired meeting they wanted with the Luciano family.

Now Frank Costello was in charge, and he always wanted to increase the family's involvement in lucrative financial schemes. He was less interested in brutality and intimidation than most gangsters. He believed more in diplomacy and discipline. He was nicknamed "the Prime Minister of the Underworld" because he controlled much of the New York waterfront and had tremendous political connections. He knew he could get a huge piece of the Catalanos' *pie* and so agreed to finally meet with their administration.

After pouring himself another shot of cognac, Giancarlo got the word that a meeting was set. As his crew began to enter his study one by one, he noticed that Ricky and Eddy were still not there. Time was going by, and everyone was waiting.

"Spitz! Get those two *stronzos* on the phone now!" Giancarlo commanded. "What the fuck is going on with those two dumb fucks?" he continued.

"Somethin' ain't right, Cat," Sammy admitted.

Just as Sammy was about to dial the telephone, the two soldiers walked into the study.

"Where the fuck you two been lately?" demanded Giancarlo. Ricky and Eddy looked at each other, both seeming hesitant to answer. Jack intervened, frustrated.

"Okay, now that we're all here, let's just get this fuckin' show goin' already." When the crew began to talk about the upcoming meeting with the Luciano family, Ricky and Eddy became visibly agitated and disturbed.

What if the rest of them found out about their extra-curricular activity? Especially Giancarlo, knowing that they had partnered with his daughter-in-law, would make him ferocious. They knew full well the wrath of the Catalano boss. But they were in it too deep now. They wouldn't be able to backtrack to justify how they started this enterprise in the first place without the boss's consent.

Ricky was particularly distressed with having had sex with Rose. Even Eddy didn't know about it, but it was weighing in on Ricky's mind so much, he began to sweat of tension. What the hell did he do? he pondered. It wasn't enough he was going behind Cat's back, earning money Giancarlo knew nothing about, but that he had sex with his boss's daughter-in-law. His own wedding was just a few short weeks away.

"Hey, Boss, I ain't feelin' so good. I need to go." Ricardo always referred to Giancarlo as *Boss*. As he walked out the door, the rest of the crew watched him, perplexed by his sudden exit. Even Eddy didn't know what to say or do but then quickly emphasized, "Yeah, Boss, even I haven't been feelin' too good lately. I think there is somethin' going around."

"What? You too now?" remarked Giancarlo, looking annoyed at him.

"Nah, don't worry, Boss. I ain't leavin'. Just wanted to tell ya."

That night, Rose lay in her bed, knowing that her two business partners were just a couple of floors down with her father-in-law. She became very agitated, but her vanity took over, and she calmed herself down by believing nothing was going to happen. She loved the control she seemed to have—control over the girls, the business, and especially over her father-in-law's two *soldiers*. What was even more exciting was the control she had over Ricky sexually. As soon as she began to feel relaxed, Rose realized Manny wasn't home yet.

Rose had cheated on her husband. This was nothing new though. She had cheated on Luca, her ex-lover, with Manny. Was he doing the same thing these days? They hadn't had sex in so long. Manny was a man—a good-looking, healthy, and sexual man who loved sex just as much as she did. But he wasn't having sex with her. He must be getting it somewhere else.

Rose began to think about the men she encountered at the bar. The men who were there to meet her "girls" were of all shapes and sizes, even those like her husband. The thought of Manny having sex with a prostitute made her furious. How could he do that? But what if he was having an affair with someone in particular? All these thoughts began to torment her mind although she had done the same thing. She justified her own actions by convincing herself it was only sexual, not emotional.

Manny had distanced himself from his wife so much and so quickly. Rose knew in her gut, that his heart belonged to someone else. For him, it was emotional and not sexual. Just as her mind began racing with anguish, she heard the door open. It was Manny. As she closed her eyes to pretend to sleep, a vision of her sister, Lili, came to her.

Lilith! Oh, how she loathed her sister.

Oh dio! Rose froze in her bed. It was her! That's who Manny was in love with. She never forgot the way he looked at her. Now looking back, it was around the time he met Lili that his demeanor toward Rose changed. Yes, he still married *her*, but now, everything was starting to make sense.

When Manny slipped under the covers, he was convinced Rose was sleeping. They shared a bed only to appear they were a normal newlywed couple. But the truth was they didn't share any real intimacy right from the start of their marriage. Rose refused to acknowledge this at the beginning, but as each day passed, Manny's true feelings for her had become clear.

To test her husband, Rose decided to try and seduce him to challenge his reaction. Even if they did have sex, she would know if it was only sexual or if their lovemaking was emotional. When she turned over to place her arm around him, she slowly started to caress her husband. She began kissing the back of his neck and placed her hand to cup his penis and gently fondle his manhood. Rose was getting aroused and thought she felt him getting an erection. But then he pushed her hand away and claimed, "I'm tired, Rose! Get some sleep."

Rose turned over and curled up in a fetal position like a little child. Before the tears started to stream, her rage had flushed her whole body.

How dare he turn me down? I'm his wife! She was exasperated. The tears began to flow, wetting her face and running down her neck.

Rose quivered uncontrollably, and Manny felt her body convulse. It was at that point he realized that his coldness toward her was not his wife's fault. He knew she loved him to a degree. Yet he was her meal ticket to America. Nonetheless, this was his wife now, and he felt maybe he had been a little too harsh toward his new bride. After all, she hadn't really done anything to deserve all this resentment from him or his family.

The next morning, both Rose and Manny awoke at the same time.

"Good morning, Rosie." Rose was brushing her hair when she turned and looked at him in complete astonishment. "Do you want to do something together today?" he inquired.

What the hell happened to him this morning? she wondered. The two of them had not done anything together as a couple in a long time. Although she was involved in a new venture, she had never felt more isolated than in this past period of her life. Whatever had come over Manny, Rose didn't want to know and didn't ask. The fact that he seemed to be coming around was enough for her.

"Yes, of course, that would be very nice." She beamed.

Finally, she had her husband back. Now she could focus on becoming the posh, chic wife of an American soldier who happened to be a Catalano, the one and only son of the Catalano fashion empire.

Manny decided to show his wife the streets of Brooklyn Heights. As they walked, he recounted his childhood memories. To Rose, it felt like they were reacquainting themselves even though they had been married for a few months now. After walking for a while, they decided to have lunch together at a local Italian café. It was known as a meeting place for new local Italian immigrants.

Rose was so proud and impressed with her husband. Everyone seemed to know him and respect him. Not only was he the son of Giancarlo Catalano of the Catalano Fashion House, but he also fought for his country. What an honor it was to finally be introduced as his wife to many of the locals. Most people knew Manny had gotten married, but few knew who she was. Now he was beginning to *show her off.*

"Hello, gorgeous, I remember you," a rather unsightly, disheveled small man smirked in his broken English. When he stared at Rose and winked, Manny quickly rose from his chair and warned him, saying, "That is my wife. Get away from here before there are problems." As others began shouting at the man to leave, Rose froze in her chair with panic and horror.

"I'm sorry, signore. I mistake her for someone else," he stuttered as he walked away. She knew exactly who he was. She remembered him coming to the bar a couple of nights a week to hustle her girls.

Oh dio! He recognized me! she fretted. How could one of those guys be there? In Brooklyn Heights! The bar was so far away.

Ricardo and Eduardo had purposely looked for a bar far enough that no one from their neighborhood would be familiar with that vicinity. Still, this was way too close to home. Just when she thought she could finally relax and start enjoying her newfound affection, a reminder of the rigid road she had decided to take recently quickly soured her emotions.

Although Rose was making great money, this was the first time she had come to regret the grim path she had selected.

Prostitution? How could I? She wept.

"Rosie, it's okay. Don't pay attention to these ignorant people," Manny reassured her. But that wasn't why she began to weep. It was more out of fear than indignity.

"Let's just go home, my love," she urged. Manny was perplexed by her term "my love"; however, he understood her eagerness to reverse their relationship.

CHAPTER EIGHT

Lili's face radiated with exhilaration every time she looked down on her baby boy. Gian-Paolo was now the essence of her universe, the only important element of her life. Nothing and no one mattered anymore. As she placed him into the wooden hand-carved cradle made by Luca, Lili recognized that her son would be the only recipient of her complete love and devotion from now on. Although Luca was a wonderful man, even he could be capable of betraying her.

If her own sister was capable of deceiving and abandoning her, no one was to be trusted. Lili cautioned herself. Rose was nine years old when Lili was born and ten years old when their parents married. But why did all that matter? Gian-Paolo was her whole life now.

Lili put Gian-Paolo down to nap when Luca answered the door to receive a letter. He brought it to the kitchen without saying anything to his wife. Although he recognized it was for Lili, he was very curious as to who it was from. So Luca took it upon himself to read it. It was from Rose. As much as she had betrayed him, he was still in love with her; a part of him still longed for her even though he realized they were not meant to be together. Maybe his fondness for Lili was not so much her appeal but retaliation for what Rose had done to him.

What Luca began to read was dreadful. How could Rose send such a heinous composition after everything Lili had been through? Although he realized Rose wasn't aware of what had transpired in the recent months, this was her sister. Or was she? He had come to learn of Rose's disdain for Lili. As he continued to read, he became aghast. Yet how could she be so callous and insensitive? The letter was devastating and heartless.

> Lilith, I am aware of the situation concerning my mother and her husband. But as you know, my life is in America now with my husband! I want no part of the past or of the deceptions exhibited during our childhood. Perhaps it is time you moved on with your life also. Omit the past! Dahlia was my mother, yes, but Paolo was never my father! Just so you are justly informed, neither Dahlia nor Paolo were your parents! My mother took you in when you were rejected and handed over to the sisters at Casa Maria Immaculata. You were a bastard child. You and I were never sisters. Please do not waste any more of your time concerning yourself with me or our fictitious family.

How could he have ever loved such a wicked woman? Her name suited her. She may have been named Rose, but she had more thorns than anyone he had ever met. What would Lili do if she ever found out this revelation? He couldn't imagine how much more devastation this poor, innocent girl could endure. But was she so innocent? After all, she had the child of another man.

Life was nothing but a series of betrayals and heartache, Luca pondered. He, too, had suffered many ravages in his life. He felt so emasculated. He was never able to join the army, never able to perform sexually; he lost his family and lost his one true love, Rose, and would never be able to produce his own children. Lili had given birth to another man's child, and he was caring for him, like his own, as to not bring shame to his wife.

What kind of man allowed his pride and dignity to be deflated by society like this? When he began to weep, Lili shouted from the bedroom, "Luca! What is wrong?" As she rushed into the kitchen to see what was going on, he quickly hid the letter in his trousers.

"Nothing is wrong, really. I just wish life was easier for us." He sniffled. Lili turned and went back to her baby in the bedroom.

Luca realized that even his beloved wife had no affection for him any longer. He was just a facade for her illegitimate infant and bogus marriage. Aside from suffering a deep dejection and despair, Luca became furious and offended. It was time he was no longer weak and pathetic. He was always somewhat insecure, but Rose had thoroughly stripped him of his honor and ego. Lili giving birth to another man's child completely plagued his insecurities.

The next morning, the sun was shining through the translucent covers. The baby's cries awoke Lili as she instantly jumped from her bed.

"Luca." She nudged her husband to get up. "I am going to take the baby for a walk this morning."

"Yes, okay. How long will you be?" he asked without any mistrust. Luca was used to Lili wandering off on her own with her baby, taking long strolls and not returning for several hours.

"I will go into town to get some things, so I might be awhile," Lili confirmed.

The mornings were usually her time alone with her son to reflect and find peace. She would remember the times she would hide out in her beloved father's little abandoned vessel by the port. It was only a few months ago, and yet it seemed like so many years had passed. So much had happened since. It seemed none of that mattered anymore. Her son was the core of her being. No one nor anything would ever cripple her again as long as she had Gian-Paolo.

After four hours of strolling, shopping, and conversing with some of the other townsfolk, Lili decided to head home. An uneasy feeling came over her. She hesitated to walk up the long stretch of driveway leading up to the house. Something didn't seem right. Luca's vehicle was gone. After entering the home, she instantly perceived echoes of emptiness. A chill and intense fear came over her whole body.

"Oh dio!" she shrieked so loudly, her son began to wail. Not only had she been stricken with fear, but she had inflicted terror on her poor baby. As she sank to the floor with her son in her arms, Lili realized Luca was gone. He had taken all his belongings and other possessions that belonged to his mother and aunt who owned the home. Once again, Lili was abandoned.

After everything that had happened to her, now this? Lili quickly composed herself, and surprisingly, a sigh of relief came over her. There were so many questions she knew would go unanswered. Where did he go? Portici? He still had his apartment there. Did he leave the house for her and her son? How long would they be able to stay there? All this speculation was overwhelming. She knew she would be fine. She had her son. That's all that mattered now. If Luca came back to reclaim the home, she would go seek Sister Margherita for help.

Lilianna spent the next few days in the house. She had enough food and supplies, so she didn't need to leave for a while. It was just her and her son. While Gian-Paolo slept, she would organize her things in such a way that should she have to up and leave quickly, everything would be ready to go.

The thought of going somewhere else again terrified her.

I could always go back to Portici, she pondered. After all, her parents' apartment was still there, sitting empty. But did she really want to go back to that chattering town, especially as a single mother now?

She didn't want to think about it. She vowed to take care of her son first and foremost and keep the house in order, with the fear that Luca or his aunt would soon come to reclaim it; she didn't want anyone to say she had left it like a pig pen, especially since there were so many rumors circulating as it was.

For many days she didn't enter the room where Luca slept. The day came when she realized she had better keep it up to par with the rest of the house. There was nothing left other than the bed and dresser, but she wanted to make sure he hadn't left anything behind. While looking through the drawers, she came across an envelope, an envelope she was hesitant to open, but her instincts expressed otherwise. Inside, she found the letter.

There it was, all the evidence and confirmation of Rose's animosity. After reading everything her malicious sister had written, Lili became paralyzed. How could anyone be so cruel? Was she that venomous she would fabricate such a vile story? Lili's fragile and inexperienced life had gone through so much turmoil in the past few months she couldn't even cry anymore. It seemed like she had reached the maximum supply of tears any human being could possibly shed. Lili was numb and dazed. This was why Luca walked away—walked away from all the havoc and carnage these two women had inflicted in his life.

Lili knew Luca had read the letter. She was also cognizant of his feelings for Rose. She was his first real love. Now everything was starting to make sense. He never truly got over the hurt Rose caused him or the agony Rose caused Lili. Maybe this was his way of paying back—setting Lili free and retaliating against Rose. If this was vengeance, Lili knew Luca wasn't finished.

After a sleepless night, Lili decided to take her son to Caserta. She took what little money she had left to purchase a train ticket. Rose's letter stated Lili was abandoned by her parents and left with the sisters at Casa Maria Immaculata. Sister Margherita would tell her the truth. But why didn't she tell her everything when she and Luca had already visited her?

After arriving at the convent, Lili was greeted by a couple of the Sisters and led inside. With her son in her arms, Lili was exasperated and collapsed. One of the sisters luckily captured Gian-Paolo before Lili fell to the floor. Sister Margherita then entered the room.

"Oh dio mio!" she screeched. "Help me bring her to the dormitory," Sister Margherita commanded. As they laid Lili onto a bed, Margherita took the baby and asked the rest of them to leave the room. "What has happened to you, my child?" she began sobbing as Lili opened her eyes.

Sister Margherita took a hold of Gian-Paolo when Lili began to wail. She had no more tears to shed, so all she could do was scream.

"Now, now, my child! Calm yourself! You are scaring your child!" Margherita demanded. Lili realized she was probably right and sat herself up. Still weeping, she looked up at the sister.

"Why did you not tell me that Dahlia and Paolo were not my parents? Why? Why didn't you tell me the truth the last time?" She found herself starting to wail again.

Sister Margherita's heart was crumbling. She had promised Dahlia never to reveal this secret. However, seeing Lili in such despair, Margherita was torn. How could a servant of God betray her like that? After asking the Lord and Dahlia to forgive her, Sister Margherita decided to tell Lili the truth.

"My dear child, these years have been very boisterous times. I loved Dahlia like my own. She was an amazing woman, and don't ever forget this. I promised her never to tell you this particular matter. She loved you so much. Perhaps it was because of this Rose was always so resentful." Lili looked at the sister with curiosity. Margherita continued, "Perhaps now you can understand Rose's envy of you. Dahlia was Rose's natural mother, yet you were not. Rose could never accept the affection and love Dahlia and Paolo had for you."

"Rose's animosity towards me was always obvious. She reminded me every day of our lives. I could never understand how a sibling could hold such hatred towards another, but now everything is clear. She was never my sister. She is actually nothing to me."

As Lili looked into Sister Margherita's eyes, she then pleaded, "Sister, I am begging you. Please tell me who my real parents were. Why was I rejected? You must tell me. You owe me that much!" she demanded.

"Oh, my dear." As Sister Margherita lowered her face and began to sob again, she continued, "Your real mother left many, many years ago—in fact, sixteen years ago, right after giving birth to you. But you were never rejected. She just couldn't take you with her."

As Lili looked at her with bewilderment, Margherita went on to tell Lili the whole story.

Her mother was an Italian American missionary nurse working in Caserta. When she became pregnant by a married Italian doctor, she decided to give up her daughter to the sisters of Casa Maria and go back to the United States. Dahlia was cherished and loved by the sisters during her stay after Rose's birth. She agreed to take care of orphaned Lili as her own. At the same time, Dahlia Rossi also consented to an arranged marriage to Paolo Bianchi, set up by the sisters at Casa Maria.

In the end, this would benefit everyone. Dahlia would have a husband, Rose would have a father, and Lili would have a family. As loving as Dahlia and Paolo always were, Lili felt a sense of complete loss. They were already dead. She would never come to know her real mother as she was in the United States and would never discover her father since the sisters did not know who he was.

The train ride home was long, and Lili felt exasperated. Italy had brought her so much anguish and pain; she couldn't take it anymore. She couldn't wait to get home and rest. When she finally reached the house, Lili found Dr. Vittorio Conte waiting. How did he even find her? Although puzzled, she was a little relieved to see a familiar face.

Lili had known him all her life, and he adored both her and Dahlia. He was like a second father.

"Liliana, ciao," he greeted as she walked up the driveway.

"Dotto, what are you doing here?"

"I wanted to see how you were and to give you these." Lili looked at the papers the doctor handed over to her but was confused.

"Please come in." After walking in together silently, she directed him to have a seat at the kitchen table.

"Liliana, I want you to look at these, but please just listen to me first before you say anything, my dear."

While looking at the documents, Lilianna realized they were annulment papers.

"Annulment?" she gasped.

"Annulment, a marriage considered to be invalid from the beginning, almost as if it had never taken place." They had been prepared by Padre Leo Marini of the Rettoria Dell'Immacolata a Cappella Reale Church in Portici. This was the parish Lili frequented as a child and the very church she and Luca married.

Lilianna slumped down into a chair next to the dottore. What did Luca say to the priest for him to agree to this annulment? The padre she poured her heart out and confessed all her sins to was the very man now ending her marriage.

Lili would go to confession at least once a week before her mother died. However, Lili stopped going to church altogether once Dahlia passed. Her biggest sins, she had never confessed. Not only did she have sex before marriage, but she also conceived a child out of wedlock. These were the sins that Padre didn't know about until now.

Lili was heartbroken and humiliated. She already concluded that Dottore Conte was aware her child was not Luca's. After all, he was the town doctor and had full knowledge of Luca's condition, but Padre Leo?

"Oh dio," she sighed.

Lili realized that everyone in Portici would probably come to learn of her illegitimate child. Luca had abandoned her and probably had returned there.

"Liliana!" Dottore Conte asserted. "There is only one thing you can do. You have no choice now. You have no family, no home, and no husband. You have no one in this dreadful place anymore, my dear. Take your son to America to be with his real father." When she looked up at the dottore in shock, he caressed her cheek and placed a kissed on her forehead.

"Go. Go, my little angel. Dahlia and Paolo would never want you to stay here and live this miserable life. They did so much for you. Now do this for them."

"How can I possibly go to America on my own? I have no one here or there!"

"Stop!" the dottore interrupted her. "I will guide and advise you, my dear. In a few days, everything will come together." Lili could not say anything after that. She was dazed.

What had happened to her in the past year? She had gone through more at her age, in a few months, than most people did in a lifetime. It was at that moment, Lili realized the doctor was right. She had nothing left. Yet she could barely manage herself in her own country, let alone in America. Lili started to panic, but then she remembered the doctor telling her to just wait a few days for him to guide her.

"You, my dear, must promise me something—if not for me, for Dahlia. She may have not been your biological mother, but she was your mother in every other sense of the word."

Lili looked at him, astonished.

How did he know this? Luca must have told him. Dottore Conte paused and stared Lili right in the eyes then continued, "Liliana, do this for your son so he may know who his real mother and father are. I will be there one day soon, my dear." Lili looked up at him with confusion. "My wife is dying. Once she is gone, I will come, and I will see you there."

Lili's eyes began to swell up with tears when Dottore Conte's somber tone changed.

"Sign these, Lilianna, and be done with your life in Napoli," he urged. After the annulment documents were signed, Dottore Conte placed his black wool-felt fedora on his head. He took the papers and leaned in to kiss Lili on the forehead once again. He then turned and walked away.

Lili sat motionless and speechless. It was Gian-Paolo's cries that quickly disrupted her hypnotic state. Holding her son in her arms, she realized he was the only thing in her life that mattered. Dottore Conte was right.

Do this for Gian-Paolo, she considered and then finally decided. Yes. It was time to start a new life. It was also time for Lili to expose her Lilith demon persona to Rose.

Her sister's contempt had finally taken its toll on Lili, and she was ready to turn the tables.

She's not even my sister. She's nothing to me now, so I do not owe her anything, especially loyalty, Lili reflected. Thinking back on the horrible and vindictive manners in which Rose conducted herself toward Lili made her cringe. Still, the thought of seeing Rose again one day petrified her.

Lilianna gathered all her belongings. She had already organized everything should she need to vacate suddenly. She would not wait for someone to come, like Luca or his aunt, to reclaim the home. Luca would never come back to her. She knew for certain her life with him was over. It was time for her to go.

Lili would remind herself that she needed to be patient for Dottore Conte to guide her. As the days passed, she waited patiently. She would wait to get further instructions from her only trusted friend, the dottore.

Of course, it wasn't long before everyone in town would come to know that Lilianna Marchese abandoned her husband while he was out of town working and stole the baby. This was one aspect of Italy should would never miss, the gossip and chatter. Once she was in America, she would never look back. Just like Rose, she would abandon her old life and forget the past. This time, Lili, too, would be going to America. She couldn't wait any longer.

Lilith! She so despised her nickname. Lili vowed that one day she would give Rose legitimate reasons for labeling her this dangerous demon. "You, my dear Rose, have spawned my conscience into the seething snake you always thought I really was," Lili fumed to herself. From this day forward, she promised herself never to have any remorse for Rose again. She would make no apologies to anyone, especially Rose, for what she was about to do or who she was about to become.

CHAPTER NINE

Everything was going well with the newlyweds. Rose tried to back away from the enterprise she had started, but would Ricky and Eddy agree? She was responsible for the girls, so the two men knew the business would collapse without her. The money flow was too profitable. They probably couldn't let this go. Still, Rose had to find a way to get out of it. She couldn't take the chance of Manny and especially his father finding out about their operation. If Giancarlo ever discovered that the three of them were involved in a secret venture not approved by him, there would be major consequences.

Rose had no doubts she could get Ricky to back down. Ricky insistently changed his mind at the threat of their liaison being exposed. Eddy was a different story. He loved not only the supply of cash but also the supply of girls.

"We have to meet," Rose demanded.

"Yeah, yeah, I know! Fuck!" Ricky snapped. He knew Rose was right. All this had to end. Ricky agreed to meet her one night at the gentlemen's club. The time had come to make some serious decisions about everything.

During their after-hours meeting, the two of them had sex again. They knew it was wrong, but it was so sexy and intoxicating. Rose and Ricky were addicted to each other sexually. Manny was becoming a wonderful husband but lacked sexual desire. Mara was too busy with the wedding plans to give her fiancé any consideration.

After their raw, exotic session of barbaric sex, they decided to get right down to business.

"We have to dissolve all this, Ricardo!" Rose badgered.

Ricky shouted back, "What the fuck am I going to do with Eddy? He said that if we pull out, he'll tell the boss. Tell him it was you and me, and we have many clients who would rat to the boss and confirm it!"

Ricky was in a state of panic when Rose said something that completely bewildered him.

"Then we must get rid of him," Rose ordered.

"What the fuck you just say?"

"You heard me, Ricardo. He must disappear."

"Rose! What the fuck you want me to do? Whack him? Are you fucking crazy or what? He's my best friend and a soldier. They'll whack me and you if they ever found out we did this!"

"They'll whack us anyway if we don't!" Rose retorted. "Would you rather they find out about us or have him disappear?"

Ricardo had been involved in plenty of illegal and criminal activities, but murder was never one of them. The Catalanos steered cleared of these extremes. Their involvements were more illegal gambling, loan sharking, extortion, protection rackets, and labor racketeering. Although the garment business was very lucrative, it was a front for the many other activities. Murder was not Crazy Cat's modus operandi. He was crazy but not that crazy.

Ricky made a call.

"Hey, Tommy Boy. It's Richie, from Brooklyn."

Tommy Burke was an Irish hit man. Many of the Italian wiseguys used him to do their dirty work. It was a better way of not allowing any connections to get back to them.

When it came to making money, Tommy was more than obliged to do the work.

"Hey, Richie, my man, to what do I owe the privilege of this call?" Ricky always used the alias Ritchie with outsiders. With the

FBI cracking down on organized crime, most soldiers and associates did whatever they could to steer the feds in the wrong direction.

"I need you to meet me in Newark. Tonight," Ricky urged.

"Newark? Ain't that a little out of your vicinity?" Tommy questioned.

"Just meet me at the Broad Street Gentlemen's Club at ten o'clock sharp," Ricardo demanded then hung up the telephone.

"What time will he be here?" Eddy questioned anxiously.

"At ten o'clock, relax." Ricky sounded irritable.

"I can't believe that bitch wanted me whacked. Me? I want to wipe this floor with that whore's ugly face!" Eddy raged as he spit on the ground.

"Calm the fuck down, you crazy fuck! Or you'll have us all killed!" Ricardo warned. "Jesus Christ! Do you realize what would happen if anyone ever found out about all this shit? She's the *Cat's* daughter-in-law too, for Christ's sake!"

"Hey, Ritchie, my *rawny* lad," Tommy greeted him sarcastically. Ricky, while staring at him, introduced him to Eddy.

"This is Tommy Boy from Bay Ridge."

"Hey." Eddy put out his hand, glaring at him.

"Your guys okay with this?" Eddy continued.

"Okay with what?" Tommy asked, confused.

"You know, your boss. He okay you with doin' business with us?" Eddy questioned.

"I don't have a boss. I freelance," Tommy stated, but before he could continue, Ricky intervened.

"Hey, boys, hate to break the party up, but there'll be no business for now. Tommy, I'll get back to you when I need you. Just don't ask any questions." Tommy and Eddy both looked at Ricardo, perplexed.

"What the fuck is goin' on?" fumed Eddy.

"Here's two hundred bucks for your time. Now get the hell out of here," Ricky asserted while nudging Tommy out the door.

As Tommy exited the room, Eddy became furious.

"What the fuck was that? I thought we were going to have the bitch whacked?"

Ricky couldn't help but roar at Eddy, "I changed my mind, you dumb-ass fuck!" He continued, "We'll figure out another way, but this can't happen. We'd be signing our own fucking death wish!" blasted Ricky.

"That bitch wanted me whacked! Fucking whore! I'll get her back somehow though." Eduardo was seething, but Ricardo knew this was an unacceptable idea.

Giancarlo was sitting in his study, sipping his usual Courvoisier cognac. Something didn't sit right, and he was feeling agitated. He wanted to move forward with the Sicilians, but not all members of his crew seemed to be reliable. He called in his trustworthy underboss and consigliere to join him—Sammy "Spitz" Spinelli, his commander, and Giacomo "Jack" Moretti, his lawyer. They were the only two people in his life he trusted wholeheartedly.

When the three men finally sat down, Giancarlo questioned Sammy and Jack, "What's going on with the Sicilians? Why I haven't I heard anything?"

"Because you asked those two *cafones* to set things up," snarled Sammy. "Hey, no disrespect, Cat. I know one of them dumb fucks is gonna be your son-in-law soon, but they're as useless as a bag of fuckin' rocks."

"Don't remind me!" Giancarlo snapped back.

"Where the fuck they been these days anyway," inquired Jack then continued, "I don't know, Cat. They haven't been good earners lately, and they're never around. Somethin's up."

Giancarlo fumed as he poured himself another drink. "I want you to call Vinny to check things out again. I'm not liking all this shit lately. Instead of progressin', we're regressin', and it's pissing me off!"

Vincent Gallo was a behind-the-scenes soldier they used as their *spy* and investigator. Giancarlo ordered him to *investigate* Eddy and Ricky to see what they were up to. At the door was Gabrielle, who entered the studio. She handed him a telegram. It stated "urgent" and simply said, "You have a grandson. Come to Portici, Napoli, to know more, and I will meet you as soon as you arrive."

Giancarlo was at a loss of words. He didn't know what to make of this news. He had a grandson? Of course, he knew it was Manny's son since he had just been in Italy, fighting in a war. He had to go over there as soon as possible. His gut feeling convinced him this wasn't an antic.

Giancarlo turned to Jack and Sammy, who had sat quietly while he read the telegram. He looked up at them and announced, "Boys, there is something I need to do. I'm going to Italia." Both men looked at each other in confusion. Giancarlo continued, "I need to find a transatlantic flight though. I won't take an ocean liner. That takes too long, and I gotta be there soon."

"Wait. What the hell is going on, Cat?" blurted Jack.

"I don't even know what the fuck is going on!" Giancarlo retaliated then went on. "I need you guys to get Vinny on our two boys and find out what the fuck they're doing. I need to go to Italy to check out my own shit! Sammy, you work with Vinny, and, Jack, I may need you to come with me."

"You know I will, but you need to tell me what the fuck for," Jack sputtered.

"Never mind. Just book a ticket for me as soon as possible. I'll go alone. I don't care how much it costs, but no ship! I don't care if I have to take two or three planes to get there!"

"Sure, Cat. I'll get right on it," agreed Jack.

Giorgia never interfered in her husband's affairs. She was the typical wealthy yet docile and submissive gangster wife. Whatever Giancarlo wanted and did, Gigi had no choice but to accept. However, this was one time she could not contain her curiosity.

"Giani, what's all this about you going to Italy?"

Looking at her sternly, Giancarlo explained, "It's business, Gigi. Now that the war is over, I can look at gettin' more fabric and ideas for distribution. What better place than the motherland?" He smiled as she raised her one eyebrow, glaring back at him with suspicion.

Giorgia was accustomed to her wealthy lifestyle by now. In no way would she jeopardize her affluent way of living. If it meant doing whatever her husband demanded, then Gigi was more than happy to oblige.

Giani and Gigi were the quintessential affluent and prominent gangster couple. They made no apologies or excuses for their lavish tastes—especially Gigi; she was one of New York's top socialites.

Given that her husband had a successful garment business meant she had access to every fashion trend and accessories. Unfortunately, the war put a halt to her accessibility. Regardless, mother and daughter, Mara, were still considered New York's top fashionistas. Although Ricardo was one of her husband's soldiers, Giorgia was never fond of her daughter's impending marriage to this type of man, given their status.

To Giorgia, her daughter, Mara, deserved far better than this simple, mediocre tough guy. Her dream was for her daughter to marry an upper-class, educated blue blood like her husband or son. With Gigi, it was all about appearances and reputation. This was the main reason Giorgia did not participate in her daughter's wedding plans and left Mara to plan it on her own.

Sitting in his studio, awaiting word on his departure arrangements, Giancarlo was anticipating the idea of a possible grandson. He couldn't believe this could be true; however, he had to find out for sure. He wanted to especially know the mother of his grandson. Giancarlo could tell from the beginning that Manny was not in love with his new Italian bride. As soon as he got word of his son's child, Giancarlo knew there was someone else who had captured Manny's heart and, obviously, mind.

Interrupting Giancarlo's trance were his consigliere and underboss, Jack and Sammy, entering the studio.

"Hey, Cat, you look like shit. What's up with you? Did you find out already?" Sammy blurted.

"Find out what? What do you know?" demanded Giancarlo.

"Take it easy. Just calm the fuck down," scolded Jack.

Jack became puzzled but continued, "We have to be careful how we're going to handle this!"

"Handle what? My grandkid?" Giancarlo snapped.

"Grandkid? What the fuck you talkin' about, Cat?" demanded Jack.

"Giacomo! What the fuck you talkin' about?" Giancarlo retorted.

As all three men looked at one another, bewildered, Vincent Gallo entered the studio.

"We brought Vinny with us, Cat. He's been waitin' outside the door. He's here to explain to you everything that's goin' on," affirmed Jack.

"What do you mean, what's goin' on? What the fuck would he know about Italy?" Giancarlo questioned.

Jack stared at him for a few seconds then, perplexed, added, "Cat, Italy? What the fuck has Italy got to do with anything? It's about those two *cafones*! You know, one of them is gonna be your son-in-law soon, remember?"

In all his adult and professional life, Giancarlo had never felt as silly or as embarrassed as he was at that moment. He was so consumed by the thought of his grandson he had completely forgotten about Vinny being hired to investigate Ricky and Eddy.

"Holy fuck! Sorry, guys. My mind's been fucked up lately with so much bullshit. I almost forgot about that shit."

"With all due respect, Cat, you're not gonna like what I have to tell ya," cautioned Vinny, "but this is somethin' you gotta know as soon as possible. Gotta take care of it before more people find out, especially the other families."

"What the fuck you talkin' about? Other families?" Giancarlo demanded.

"Cat, just listen to what he's gotta say, and then we'll have to make some decisions," Jack interjected.

"Your two goons have been earnin' on the side," Vinny stated.

"What the fuck you just say?" Giancarlo snapped. "Earnin'? They haven't been doin' shit!"

"For you, no!" interrupted Vinny. "But for themselves, they've been making some pretty damn good coin."

"What the fuck!" Giancarlo raged.

Vinny continued to explain to the boss about the prostitution enterprise they had going in New Jersey. Giancarlo was seething at the thought of his two soldiers doing business without his consent. Ricky was his soon to be own son-in-law.

Vinny was hesitant to continue when he had to reveal to Giancarlo his daughter-in-law was the mastermind behind the operation. However, that's what he was hired to do, so he did.

"Your spicy Italian daughter-in-law is the *capo* of this whole operation—actually, *capa*, I should say. She's in charge of all the girls."

After Vinny relayed all the information, Giancarlo became enraged. There was no way he could let them continue making a fool of him, not his soon-to-be son-in-law nor his daughter-in-law. She was already part of the family—however, not for long, he promised.

"Sammy, I want you to have a chat with Tommy Burke, that Irish kid from Bay Ridge."

Sammy knew right away what the Cat was referring to. Giancarlo had never gone to this extreme. Wanting Tommy involved meant he was going to take the further steps many of his peers took when necessary.

"You guys take care of those two fucks, but don't you dare touch my daughter-in-law. I will take care of that conniving little bitch myself! It's not enough she conned my son, but she wanted to make a fuckin' *stronzo* outta me?" Giancarlo fumed.

The other men had never seen him this angry. He was usually the calm and composed one. But this? Sammy spit on the carpet. This was the ultimate betrayal, and it was from a woman.

Just as the men were leaving, Manny and Rose entered the house. After spending the day together, Rose never seemed happier. She had finally gotten her husband to appreciate her. Yet her deceit behind her father-in-law's back would always lurk in the depths of her mind.

The venture was exciting at first, but she wanted no part of it anymore. She just wanted to be like her mother-in-law, Giorgia—a wealthy, respected socialite whose main role was to dress well and attend all the social events she could possibly handle.

This was the life Rose had always envisioned. Not as a madame in charge of call girls running a brothel. Prostitution had become a normal enterprise back in Italy during the war. Rose always knew her mother, Dahlia, was tangled within that netting. Of course, Dahlia would never ever mention anything to her daughters.

Lilianna may have been too young and naive to notice, Rose thought to herself, but she was the older, smarter one who knew better.

Rose had a deep resentment not only for Lili but also for her mother. Aside from the prostitution, she could never understand why Dahlia displayed much more love and compassion for Lili, a little girl who was not her flesh and blood. To Rose, Dahlia was all she had since she did not know her father, yet her own mother preferred another child.

How could I lower myself to the same standards as those peasants in Italia? Rose fumed. How could she have possibly gotten herself into the prostitution trade? The same occupation she loathed back home was the same venture she was now operating. *No! This must end,* Rose grunted. She was in America. She was married to a handsome GI who was also very rich. All her dreams had come true. How could she destroy all this with a risky business?

The thought of Giancarlo or Manny finding all this out made Rose nauseous and hysterical. Since the beginning, she had experienced bouts of anxiety and dread. However, since her marriage was going well, she was determined to put an end to it. Rose already knew Ricardo was onboard, but it was Eduardo they had to take care of. He was the only one obstacle that needed to be erased.

"Hey, Manny boy, how's the man?" Tommy walked up to shake his hand.

"Fine but tired." Rose could tell by the look on Manny's face that he was not fond of this person. "Good night, guys," Manny added, leading Rose by the arm up the stairs. Giancarlo stared at Rose with a look of disgust as they walked by. Rose noticed her father-in-law's scowling face and became alarmed.

Why did he look at me that way? she fretted.

Once she and Manny entered their room, she quickly queried, "Why were you so cold with that gentleman, my darling?"

"He is no gentleman, believe me," corrected Manny. "He is just a stupid, ruthless Irishman from Bay Ridge. Tommy Burke, what a piece of shit! What the fuck was he doing here?" ranted Manny as he stared at Rose, puzzled. She herself was puzzled. The name sounded very familiar.

Tommy Burke? Oh dio mio! Rose knew that name. Ricky had mentioned it the night they were together. He was the man they were going to hire to get rid of Eddy. *What is he doing here? Why aren't Ricky or Eddy here? What the hell is going on?* Rose panicked. As she lay in her bed, her mind and heart began racing beyond control. She couldn't sleep at all. Everything was so confusing, and to think of it, she hadn't seen Ricky in awhile. He was supposed to take care of Eddy, she pondered.

The first thing Rose did the next morning was telephone Ricky. He barely finished saying hello when she shrieked, "I have to see you as soon as possible!"

"Wait, what the fuck is the urgency? And where the fuck is your husband?" snapped Ricky.

"Manuele is in Manhattan, so meet me at our place! Now! We need to talk!" demanded Rose.

"What a crazy-ass broad," Ricky grumbled to himself. "How the fuck did she con me into all this bullshit?"

When Ricky entered the office at the gentlemen's club, Rose was already there, in a state of shock and hysteria.

"Calm the fuck down!" Ricky ordered. "Stop with your gibberish. How the hell can I help you if you don't tell me what the fuck is going on?" Rose stared at him for few seconds in distress.

"Why was that Tommy Boy at the house last night? Did you tell anyone of our plan concerning Eddy?" rasped Rose.

"Wait just a fuckin' minute. What the fuck you babblin' about? Tommy was at Cat's place?" retorted Ricky.

"Yes! I know he is the boy you called to take care of Eddy. He is Tommy Burke from Bay Ridge, right?" stuttered Rose.

Ricky became agitated and concerned. He hadn't spoken to anyone in the crew about Tommy other than Eddy. What was he thinking, calling him in front of Rose? He had no intention of ever getting rid of Eddy. He just made her believe that. But then he and Eddy decided it would be Rose who would be disposed of.

Did Eddy tell the crew members and the boss? No way, he speculated. If Eddy had said anything about Rose, then they would also find out about their extracurricular activities, and Eddy wasn't that dumb.

Ricky was on the phone with Eddy immediately after Rose left.

"Get your fuckin' filthy ass over here right now! We need to discuss a few matters!" Without hesitation, Eddy was there in no time.

"What the fuck's goin' on?" Eddy snarled.

"Did you know anythin' about our friend from Bay Ridge visitin' the Crazy Cat?" demanded Ricky.

"What? What the fuck you talkin' about? When was he with the Cat?" Eddy was stunned, and based on his reaction, Ricky knew right away he had no idea himself. He had known Eddy long enough to know when he was lying or telling the truth.

"How you know he was visitin' with him?" urged Eddy.

"That crazy-ass guinea brat was just here! She said he was at the place last night!" raged Ricky.

"If he was there, you know what that means? Someone's gettin' whacked! Sons of bitches didn't even include us in the meetin'!"

"What are we gonna do?" Eddy gulped.

"Nothin'! We just wait and watch. Somethin's up, and I'm gonna find out about it."

Ricky looked over at Eddy. He could see the fear in Eddy's face and quickly reassured him, "Hey, don't worry, kid. I'm in the family. He's gonna be my father-in-law soon. He ain't gonna do shit to us. Trust me."

Rose's heart was beating fast, and she could hardly breathe. When she walked in the door and began going up the stairs, she could hear Manny with his father in the studio. Her heart was pounding.

"Rosanna, come here." When her father-in-law requested for her to enter, she became overwhelmed with anxiety and dread. In all the months she had lived there, she had never entered the studio. After seeing his face last night, she was even more petrified than ever.

"My father is leaving tomorrow for a few days," exclaimed Manny.

"Oh? Where are you going, Signore Catalano?" stuttered Rose quietly.

"I'm going to Italia."

"Italia?" interrupted Rose.

Both Manny and Giancarlo looked at her, puzzled. They could tell by the look on her face she was nervous and agitated.

"Don't worry, my dear. I'll be back," joked Giancarlo. He was trying hard to contain his contempt for this woman who had betrayed him. But he had a plan. "I wanted to meet with both of you before I departed. I know it's been a few months since you got married, and your mother and I never had a party for the two of you. So when I get back, we'll have a real nice reception, and you'll get a real nice weddin' present."

Rose was relieved and delighted. She always wanted a special soiree to celebrate her marriage to her American GI, yet things didn't go as planned when she first arrived. Now everything was falling into place. She would buy the most beautiful gown for the occasion and get to meet all the Catalanos' fancy friends. This celebration would finally be her debut into the elite world her in-laws were part of.

When Giancarlo left for the airport, Rose couldn't help but still feel uneasy about her father-in-law. Nothing was making sense. Why was he going to Italy? Gigi had mentioned that it was for work, but something didn't add up. One night he was seething and glaring at her with disdain, and then the next he was smiling and eager to have a wedding celebration for them. He also mentioned a wedding present. What kind of gift was he thinking of giving them? Although she was excited, Rose felt uneasy. Nevertheless, she had a few days of not having to worry about her father-in-law hearing anything about her business while he was in Italy.

CHAPTER TEN

Giancarlo had never been on a commercial airline before. He boarded the United Airlines Douglas DC-6, which was originally intended as a military aircraft during the war. However, the aircraft had been modified into a long-range commercial transport airliner. He had also never been to Italy. When the plane finally touched down, he could see much of the devastation caused by the war. He had always heard his parents talk about the motherland but was grateful they had decided to immigrate to the United States.

Giancarlo was just a little boy when his family came to New York. If they had stayed, he would have been living among this ruin—if he and his family would have been lucky enough to survive all this carnage. When he exited the plane, his son, Manny, came into his mind. Although his son didn't want to follow in his father's footsteps and take care of the business, he was never so proud of him. Manny had served his country with honor and dignity and never complained to his parents about his duty.

Giancarlo felt blessed for the life he was able to build for himself in New York. He had everything a man could want—a devoted wife, loving children, abundance of friends, a lavish lifestyle, and especially a lucrative business. Even though much of his business dealings were not legitimate, he was still proud of his accomplishments.

Giancarlo was finally in his homeland to meet his grandson. To have a grandson was one of the highest honors. It was like being in a royal family with an heir to the throne. In an Italian family, it was especially important so the family name could carry on into future generations. Was this really his grandson? He had trusted some random stranger who sent him a telegram that simply stated "Come to Portici, Napoli, and I will meet you as soon as you arrive." He hesitated.

As soon as Giancarlo went through customs and had his luggage, he stood for a few minutes and became disoriented.

"Okay, so I guess I have to go to Portici now," he muttered to himself.

The train ride to Naples was three hours long, and from there, Giancarlo would board a bus to Portici that would take him another thirty minutes. It was the longest day he had ever experienced, especially with the time difference. He had never had to go through so much inconvenience his whole life. But this was for his grandson, he reminded himself.

What if this was all just a hoax or misunderstanding? When his bus reached Portici, Giancarlo was not only uncomfortable but also irritated at the idea that someone could possibly be misleading him. It wasn't enough that puttana of a daughter-in-law was deceiving him. If he was being made a fool of about this, there would be grave consequences. He already had a plan in place for Rose for when he returned home, but he had to deal with this situation first.

When he stepped off the bus, Giancarlo didn't know what to do except start walking the town. Sooner or later, someone would ask him something. As he strolled along, he couldn't help but feel troubled and somber about what he was seeing. The town was almost completely ravaged by the war. What was once a beautiful picturesque seaside town, he thought, was now only a shell. He went into a trance when a man walked right up and stood before him.

"Signore Catalano, how do you do?"

Startled, Giancarlo questioned, "Oh, you speak English? Good. How do you know who I am?" He looked at the man suspiciously.

"This is a small town, my friend. The people knew right away that an Americano had arrived. We haven't seen much of the Americans since the war ended, so of course, when one arrives, everyone knows about it. I am Dottore Vittorio Conte. I am the one who sent you the telegram." As Giancarlo stared at him with doubt, Dottore Conte continued, "Come, my friend. You can stay at my home."

There were no hotels around, as Giancarlo had already noticed. Who was this strange man he was trusting during his stay? After a sleepless night in a very uncomfortable bed, Giancarlo couldn't wait to get going.

The man is a doctor and lives under these conditions? he questioned. But then he realized, this wasn't New York. This was a country that just went through a war. This was an area of the country that had been bombarded by more warfare than any other part of the world.

Giancarlo was waiting on the front steps of the building when Dottore Conte came around the corner in his Convertible Touring Alfa Romeo 6C 2500 SS Spider MM. Now this was a car.

"He may not live in the nicest of homes, but he sure does have a beautiful car," Giancarlo mumbled to himself.

"Signore Catalano, please. Let me accompany you to someone who I think you will find quite interesting." Giancarlo didn't say a word. He simply entered the vehicle and let Dottore Conte drive him to wherever he intended.

After knocking on the door several times, a young man finally came to open it.

"Dottore Conte."

"Buon giorno, Luca. I would like you to meet someone."

"Please do come inside," Luca directed them both to the salon. He had no idea why the men were there, but Dottore Conte wasted no time telling him.

"This is Signore Giancarlo Catalano from America."

Luca looked perplexed. Why would any American come back to Portici, especially now that it was in ruins?

Before Luca could say anything, Dottore Conte continued, "This, my dear boy, is a very close acquaintance of our lovely Rosanna."

"Rose?" Luca blurted.

"Yes, Luca. In fact, this gentleman is her husband's father."

Although Giancarlo was silent the whole time, he finally roared, "Can someone please tell me what the fuck is going on? Where is my grandson? Is he even my grandson? Enough of this bullshit. Just tell me what the fuck I'm doing here!"

The dottore advised Luca to tell the American signore the whole story from the beginning—from Luca's relationship with Rosanna to his marriage to Liliana. When he reached the part about Lilianna getting pregnant, the dottore took over the story. He explained his special relationship with Dahlia and why Lili had meant so much to him. He was never fond of Rosanna and felt Lili deserved to be with the father of her child, whom she really loved.

"Holy Christ," answered Giancarlo, shaking his head. Both men looked at each other in surprise at Giancarlo's reaction. It seemed he wasn't as shocked by the revelations about Rose as they would have thought. Giancarlo was fully made aware of Rose's contempt for her sister, resentment toward her parents, betrayal of her fiancé, and manipulation of Manny.

Sadly, it didn't matter how bad or selfish Rose was; Luca always loved her regardless. No one ever understood this obsession he had for her. Even after she betrayed him, he still loved her and always hoped that one day he would see her again.

"Listen. My grandson, where is he? That's what I came for," Giancarlo declared.

"Yes, signore, I will take you to him now." The dottore quickly arose, realizing Giancarlo couldn't wait any longer. During the two-hour drive from Portici to Benevento, Giancarlo stayed calm and quiet while the dottore did all the talking. Giancarlo had taken in so much information in one morning that he had developed a headache.

When they finally reached the house and started making their way up the driveway, Giancarlo started getting tense. His heart began beating harder and harder.

Oh my god! he thought to himself. He had never felt nervousness, but this was a different kind of matter. He quickly jumped out of the car to make his way to the door.

After a few seconds, the door opened. There she was, Liliana—the girl who had given birth to his grandson, the girl who had seized her son's heart and mind. She was also the most beautiful girl Giancarlo had ever seen. She had beautiful auburn locks and mesmerizing eyes. She looked like an angel with the most delicate and stunning face. Her voluptuous curves were evident in her navy-blue polka dot swing dress.

At that moment, Giancarlo understood everything and knew what he had to do.

"Liliana, this is Signore Catalano." Giancarlo and Lili stared at each other, both in complete bewilderment. The Dottore continued, "May we come in?"

"Oh dio, forgive me, of course, please come in." Lili quickly snapped out of her daze. This was Manny's father, the man responsible for spawning the love of her life, and her son's grandfather. *He is so handsome*, she thought to herself while staring at him.

For the first fifteen minutes, there was general conversation while Lili made the men espresso. She would also bring out some of her homemade biscotti. Giancarlo was impressed by her domestic skills. He was old-school and loved a woman who knew how to keep house, cook, and bake. She seemed like the perfect young woman. Rose was nothing like her, he reflected, while sipping his coffee. Lili became very concerned by the shaking of his head several times, but when Giancarlo realized what he was doing, he reassured her, he was just thinking about things from back home.

"Liliana, my dear, Signore Catalano is here to see Gian-Paolo," asserted Dottore Conte. Lili walked out of the salon. Giancarlo looked over at him, bewildered.

"*Gian*-Paolo? She named the kid after me?"

"And after her father, Paolo," responded the Dottore. When Lili walked into the room with the little baby boy, tears began to stroll down Giancarlo's face.

Lili had placed Gian-Paolo into the arms of his grandfather. Giancarlo had never felt more humbled. With his lavish, hectic, and tumultuous lifestyle, this was the first time he had ever felt peace. Holding his grandson reminded him of the days when Manny was a baby. Gian-Paolo looked just like Manny. There was no question—this child was a Catalano.

Giancarlo had quickly decided that his grandson would go back to New York one day soon along with Lilianna. After meeting her, he knew this girl was needed and wanted back in America. That's where she belonged, not Rose.

As he held his grandson in his arms, Giancarlo began to ask Lili many questions about her life with her sister. For a girl who was normally shy, she didn't hesitate explaining everything to him. For her, it was finally a way to vent all her shortcomings and frustrations and not feel guilty about sharing intimate details. Although Dottore Conte was the only other person who knew her life story, she felt Giancarlo needed to know the truth surrounding his grandson's circumstances.

Lilianna had vowed to never recognize Rose as a sibling again. After all, she wasn't her sister, and she made sure Giancarlo became aware of this. She explained her name Lilith, labelled by Rose. Giancarlo sensed the heartache and despair in her voice as she began to weep.

Lili's anguish made him somber and furious at the same time, livid that a puttana like Rose had the audacity to call this beautiful, innocent young girl Lilith. How dare she refer to the mother of his grandson as a dangerous demon she was far from?

Lili's life was obviously full of darkness, but her soul was definitely not. Giancarlo was contemplating and reflecting on all the information he had just digested; he then quickly handed the baby over to Lili.

"Dottore Conte, we must go. I have many things to take care of. Liliana, we will keep in touch." Then Giancarlo turned to walk away. The dottore and Lili looked confused. Why did he get up so quickly and want to leave?

"Lilianna, my dear, I will be back. Don't worry, my child," reassured Dottore Conte as he, too, then walked away. Lili watched them from the door, driving away.

"My mistake, Signore Catalano," apologized the dottore.

"For what?" questioned Giancarlo. "For bringing you to Lilianna today. I know all this has been too much for you in one day." Giancarlo began to laugh.

"This was no mistake, I reassure you, my friend. But I am a businessman who realizes when an opportunity presents itself, action must be taken, or the chance will be lost." The dottore was puzzled by his response. What did business have to do with the signore meeting his grandson? Dottore Conte sensed a vibe that Giancarlo was not fond of his current daughter-in-law, Rose.

"There are a couple of things I need to do before I go back to New York, and I would like you to accompany me," asserted Giancarlo then continued. "First thing, when we go back to that shit hole of a town, I want you to bring me to the Comune di Portici. Then I need you to bring me to the Museo di Capodimonte in Naples." Dottore Conte was perplexed. Why did this American need to go to town hall and an art gallery? What did these have to do with anything?

After another sleepless night, Giancarlo had become very anxious. He had only known the dottore for a mere twenty-four hours; however, he realized quickly that he was a man to be trusted.

Giancarlo admired the dottore's compassion and affection for Liliana. He noticed their special bond. After meeting Lili himself, he could understand her allure. Even though she was actually a young girl, she was *more woman* than most he had ever met.

After a quick breakfast and short car ride, the two men entered the Comune di Portici. Giancarlo stressed to the woman at the front desk that he had to see the mayor immediately. Because he was a distinguished American whom the townsfolk had already come to know, she instantly obliged without hesitation. Gennaro Fermariello quickly emerged from his office.

"Signore Catalano, I am Sindico Fermariello."

"Yes, I know who you are." Giancarlo and the mayor shook hands.

"To what do I owe this pleasure?" the mayor inquired.

Giancarlo put his arm around the mayor's shoulders and guided him back to his office. The idea was to make sure no one was around to hear their conversation. As they closed the door behind them, Dottore Conte stared with a look of curiosity but also disappointment. He patiently waited for about thirty minutes before Giancarlo emerged from the mayor's chambers.

Although the dottore was inquisitive, Giancarlo did not disclose any details of their discussion, other than he wanted to "donate" money to the town. The dottore couldn't help but smile. He knew the American businessman had made a deal with the mayor.

What was it? He didn't know; however, it was probably a trade-off. Since Lilianna was born, the dottore's bond with her and Dahlia was so profound he considered them family.

Hopefully, his beloved Lili would finally find some happiness. The dottore was convinced Giancarlo would make sure of it.

"Okay, Doc, can you bring me to the gallery?"

"But of course, Signore Catalano," the dottore assured.

Giancarlo indicated he wanted to buy a special painting for his son and bride. When he mentioned Rose, Dottore Conte's cheery mood turned to displeasure. Giancarlo explained he was going to throw an extravagant banquet in their honour when he returned. He had not purchased a wedding gift, so he would present this exclusive souvenir to them at the reception.

Once they reached the gallery, the dottore could not help himself from asking, "Do you have something in particular in mind, signore?" Giancarlo was known to be an intelligent and cunning man. He sensed the dottore's *curiosity* from the beginning. He simply said, "Not quite sure yet, but I'll know when I'm inside. I will say it is going to be exceptional." It was then the dottore realized the American businessman was enigmatic and mysterious. This was Giancarlo's appeal to everyone who knew or met him.

After browsing around to view the many paintings, Dottore Conte could hear Giancarlo ask a young man if he could get the director of the gallery. After five minutes, a dashing gentleman presented himself.

"I am Direttore Sorrentini. How may I be of assistance?" As he did with the mayor, Giancarlo put his arm around the direttore's shoulders after shaking his hand. Once again, Giancarlo did not want the dottore to know what he was requesting. Dottore Conte then excused himself and waited outside, smoking a cigarette while the signore made yet another deal.

It didn't take long before Giancarlo emerged from the building.

"Did you find what you were looking for, Signore Catalano?"

"Yes, indeed, I did, Doc. I had to order it so they will have to ship it to me in America." Dottore looked at him in astonishment. Just how rich was this man? Not only did he fly over instead of taking a ship; he was having a unique painting shipped over?

The dottore couldn't help but feel it should have been Lili at the end of the signore's generosity, not Rose. It was no wonder Rosanna dug her claws into his son, he theorized.

After arriving home, Giancarlo thanked the dottore and his wife. He bid them both good night. The next morning, Giancarlo greeted the couple and stood at the doorway with his luggage.

"Where are you going, signore?" gasped the dottore.

"I have to go. I have a lot of work to do back home. Can you take me to the train station, Doc?" Giancarlo requested.

"But, signore, you just arrived a couple of days ago, and you want to leave already?"

"Yeah. I did what I had to do here. Now I have to go. So will you take me or not?" stressed Giancarlo.

"Of course, Signore, right away," the dottore reassured.

The two men did not say a word to each other on the way to Naples. Once they arrived, Giancarlo looked over at the dottore and handed him two envelopes.

"One of these is for you—you know, to thank you for everything that you have done. But the other one is for the girl and my grandson. I need you to do something for me." After explaining what he wanted him to do with the envelope for Lili, the dottore smiled with delight.

"Grazie, Signore Catalano. I will make sure Lili gets this. Ciao, e buona fortuna."

Several days had gone by before Dottore Conte showed up at Lili's door. The last time was with the Signore Catalano. During those days, she wept often and felt lost at the direction of her life. She had no will to leave the house; however, she knew it was time for her to go elsewhere.

When she finally heard the knock at the door, she knew instantly it was Dottore Conte. As soon as she opened it, a stream of tears began to run down her face.

"Now, now, my dear child, what is all this for? You must stop. I have come to give you amazing news." The dottore beamed. "Come, come, let's go into the salotto," he insisted.

The dottore handed Lili an envelope and continued, "Cara mia, signore Catalano wanted you to have this. He gave me specific and imperative instructions." After opening the envelope, Lili found two tickets and a substantial amount of money.

The name Liliana Bianchi was on one of the tickets aboard the MS *Volcania*. Her son's name, Gian-Paolo, was on the other. When she looked up at Dottore Conte in complete shock and confusion, he stated, "Complements of Signore Catalano." Then he encouraged her, "Lilliana, you must go."

Dottore Conte emphasized how much she needed to abandon her life in Italy and start a new one in the United States, with or without Manny. This was for her and her son. He went on to direct her, "When you reach Ellis Island, la Signora Letizia Fabbri will be there for you. You will stay with her in her home." Lifting her chin with his hand, he added, "Once you arrive, everything will be taken care of, my dear."

After a tight and lengthy embrace, the dottore drove away. Lili looked at the ticket.

"Oh dio! Tomorrow?" she blurted. The ticket indicated the date of departure. She was stunned yet relieved. She couldn't wait any longer to leave the distressing place behind. It was a site in ruins and of too many heartbreaking memories. The only person she was going to miss was the Dottore. Lili reminded herself he had said his wife was dying, and he would come the United States one day,

When she noticed all the money, she began to cry—only this time they were tears of joy. She had enough money to take care of her and her son for a long time. With this, she could get on a bus and train to Naples and board the ship. She wouldn't have to worry about not having any money left as there was plenty. Lili had already gathered her things earlier when worried she would need to vacate if Luca or his aunt reclaimed the house.

After everything was done, she took her son into the town to find out when the bus would arrive that evening. She didn't want to stay one more night in that house. She made sure she had ample time for the bus and the train so she wouldn't miss the boat the next day.

It was going to be a long eleven days, but the excitement began to flush her body to the point where she began to giggle. Lili hadn't giggled in such a long time, let alone laugh. This was not only a dream but a retaliation to Rose's malicious behaviour over the years.

That night, the bus driver agreed to meet Lili at the end of her driveway. There wouldn't be many people on the bus, and he took pity on her, knowing she lived so far from the center of town, where the bus station was located. He couldn't let this beautiful, innocent angel and her baby walk to the town with all their belongings like that. No. He wouldn't have it.

Once Lili reached the train station, she took the first train to Naples. She didn't want to waste more time than she had to, even if it meant waiting at the dock for hours. She just wanted to get to the ship and make sure she and Gian-Paolo would make it.

Once she reached the vessel, her heart began to pound.

Look at this incredible ocean liner, marvelled Lili. She had always loved the water and especially boats. She missed the days she just lay in her father's little fishing vessel. Those times brought her much peace. Now she was hoping this beautiful ship would sail her away to much-needed serenity again.

The moment had arrived for everyone to board the ocean liner. Lilianna turned around to give Napoli one last look. She vowed, even as the ship sailed away, she would not look back. Instead, she and her son would go rest and sleep—for one, because it had been a long couple of days, and two, never would she look back at her old life again. It was time to look forward.

CHAPTER ELEVEN

Although Giancarlo had only been gone for three days, it seemed like weeks to his family and crew—except for Rose. She was agitated and flustered. How could he be back so soon? Just when she finally felt relaxed, she was disturbed once again.

Why did Giancarlo go to Italia in the first place? she fretted. He did say it was for business, but Rose sensed uneasiness about the circumstances.

That night, the whole family gathered for dinner. Gabrielle and chef Dario De Santis, from Giancarlo's favorite restaurant, Villa Toscana, prepared his favourite four-course meal—caprese salad, fettuccini with mussels, followed by an assortment of deep-fried seafood, ending with zeppole and espresso. Everyone was gathered around the dining table, including Salvatore; his wife, Lucia; Giacomo; and his wife, Nella.

During dinner, Gabrielle came running out of the kitchen, frantic.

"Mr. C, there is a telephone call for you. It's urgent." Once Giancarlo took the phone, all anyone could hear from him was "What?" After he emerged from the kitchen, he looked around the table and then announced, "I'm sorry to inform everyone, but Eduardo and Ricardo, they're gone."

Mara became hysterical. "Gone? What the fuck you mean, gone?" Then she began to scream and wail.

"Gigi, bring Mara upstairs, now!" he demanded.

"Dead? Pops, what the fuck is going on? What do you mean? They're dead?" Manny questioned his father.

Rose couldn't move. While everyone began speculating their demise, she became terrified. Did someone find out about their venture? What about her part in it? Just when she started to tremble with fear, she realized this was her way out.

With Ricky and Eddy gone, Rose had no one to answer to anymore. She would be able to just abandon the gentlemen's club. It was fair enough that she would never have to go near that area again, ever. Now she could carry on with her life. After several minutes of relief, regret set in. Ricky came to mind. She couldn't believe she would never see or be with him again.

At a time when Mara was planning her wedding, she would now be helping Ricky's family plan his funeral. Giorgia would take care of all the wedding cancellations. Mara hadn't even been married yet and was already considered a widow. It broke Gigi's heart to see her daughter going through so much pain. However, even she was never enthused about Mara's upcoming nuptials. Gigi was actually relieved that the wedding wouldn't be taking place.

Right before he left for Italy, her husband, Giancarlo, had directed Gigi to start planning a reception for their son. Since she was no longer going to be part of her daughter's wedding, she could at least plan some sort of fancy soiree for her son, anything to put the family in the spotlight. Throwing a lavish reception was just what Gigi thrived on. Although postwar, everything was at a premium, money was no object for the Catalanos.

The funerals for Ricky and Eduardo were only one day apart. The family wanted to wait a respectable time frame after their deaths to hold Manny and Rose's reception. They decided to wait a few weeks before sending out the invites. Giancarlo also wanted to make sure his special gift would arrive in time. Although Gigi was concerned that her daughter, Mara, would be overshadowed at a time of mourning, she was eager for the social spotlight again.

Because of the war, Gigi hadn't hosted many parties lately. She had been known for her extravagant social gatherings but mainly amid the Italian community. The real aristocrats of New York thought of her as nothing more than a tacky gangster's wife.

Gigi never cared much for the opinions of outsiders. Her focus was on the surrounding Catalano social circle. Being on top as the finest fashionista and socialite among her peers, Gigi basked in the envy of others.

The only benefit to Mara getting married was the swanky wedding Gigi would have the pleasure of hosting. However, given the circumstances, that would no longer be. At least now she would be able to start planning another opulent banquet. But why did her children make such poor selections in their choice of spouses?

Both Giancarlo and Giorgia were usually disappointed in their children. It wasn't just in their choices for partners but in their life choices in general. Of course, they were proud of their son for enlisting and serving in the military. Yet why didn't Manny want to take over his father's business? Why did he marry a disturbing peasant girl? Why did Mara not learn to be more domestic like her mother? Since Ricky's death, all she did was sleep and party. The only thing that had kept Mara busy before were her wedding plans. Since it was no longer happening, the Catalanos worried her useless habits would become worse, and they did.

"Daddy! I want to know who killed my Ricky," demanded Mara while stumbling into Giancarlo's studio.

"Don't you think I wanna know myself, my *pupa*?" he replied. When she began to howl, Mara sat down on her father's knee, just as she did when she was a little girl. But her father realized she was inebriated. "Get up! Get the fuck up! You're fucking drunk! Go take a shower and go to bed," demanded Giancarlo. Just as he tried to hold her up, Mara collapsed. He called out to his wife and the housemaid.

Giancarlo was disheartened and crushed. Seeing his daughter in such despair and heartache was painful for him. When Gabrielle and Gigi picked Mara off the floor, Gigi glared over at her husband. Two of his soldiers had been murdered. One was his soon-to-be son-in-law. Both were shot point-blank to the back of the head, execution-style. Yet her husband had been stone-cold about the murders.

Could he have been behind them? she speculated. Gigi would never question her husband. Plus murder wasn't the Cat's style.

Both Eddy and Ricky were found dead in Newark, New Jersey, a district none of the crew, associates, or even police could figure out. Why were both men out there? It wasn't their territory. Ricky was found in the parking lot of the gentlemen's club. He had been shot in the head, and his lifeless body was found beside his car. Eddy was found with the same head wound in a bed of a cheap motel. Word got out that he had been with one of the hookers that night, but she was gone before he was killed.

Still fuming, Giancarlo poured himself a glass of cognac. It was acceptable for a man to overindulge in alcohol but not for a woman, especially his own daughter. When he sat back down in his chair, he began to contemplate as to what needed to be done next. Lately, Giancarlo had been trying hard to keep his contempt for Rose from being evident. He wanted everyone to believe he had developed a newfound affection for his daughter-in-law. But he also had a plan.

Part of Giancarlo's plan was to mentally torture Rose. He could already tell by the look on her face when he announced the deaths of Ricky and Eddy that she was horrified. But this would only be the beginning of his vengeance.

I'm going to make that little bitch puttana regret she ever stepped foot on American soil. Giancarlo scowled at the thought of Rose. How did she have the *balls* to betray him and his son?

Giancarlo seethed at the thought of Rose, but then Lili came to mind. How did his son fall for such a beautiful, innocent angel like her and end up with her shameless *slut* of a sister? Well, at least the *angel* was the mother of his grandson. Giancarlo grinned to himself.

How does that puttana have the nerve to call her sweet sister Lilith, the demon of darkness? One thing's for sure—that little girl will defi-

nitely be a demon to you one day soon, you stupid bitch! Giancarlo raged as he poured himself another cognac.

"Right this way, gentlemen," Gabrielle directed Sammy, Jack, and Vinny Gallo into the studio.

"Vinny, to what do I owe this honor? I thought our work was done?" Giancarlo said, perplexed.

"Yeah, Cat, about the gentlemen's club, I think there's somethin' else you gotta know. I didn't want to tell you until the other two were gone, but this is somethin' you gotta hear," Vinny addressed the Capo.

"What? What the fuck else? I haven't got all day," Giancarlo snapped.

"All right, take it easy. Aside from the business at the club, your daughter-in-law was also shackin' up with Ricardo."

Giancarlo didn't say a word. Everyone paused for a minute when Sammy asked, "How many other fuckin' *babbo*s she been shackin'?"

"Who knows? I only know of Ricky, and that son of a bitch was going to marry your daughter," confirmed Vinny. "That bastard was putting his dick in that puttana's twat and then in your daughter's?" Sammy spit in disgust. "If we hada known this before, we woulda had his dick chopped off first before the bullet to the head!"

"Hey! What the fuck is wrong wichu? That's my fucking daughter you're talkin' about," snapped Giancarlo.

"Sorry, Cat, you know I don't mean any disrespect. I was referring to the other twat, you know," apologized Sammy.

"Easy with the twat remarks, you fuckin' *momo*! Never put my daughter in the same category or sentence with that bitch!" ordered Giancarlo.

Sammy lowered his head in remorse when Jack intercepted, "Whata we gonna do about this club, Cat? Those bastards *went south* on us. They were skimmin' lots of cash."

"And that bitch is still in my house!" exclaimed Giancarlo while hitting his clenched fist on the desk. Giancarlo always tried to keep his cool, but lately his anger was apparent.

"We need to call Tommy Boy again?" inquired Jack.

"No. I'm going to handle this my way. Getting rid of her is way too easy. She needs to suffer." Then with a little chuckle, Giancarlo continued, "Plus my daughter is already a widow. We gonna make my son a widower?"

"I do want you to call Tommy Boy though, only not for what you think," requested Giancarlo. "We're going to do more business with him, but not the kind he's used to."

"I'm not getting' it," Sammy said, puzzled as he looked over at the rest of them.

"You want to put the club in Tommy's name," Jack stated, smiling at Giancarlo.

"You see, this is why I love you, Jackie. You always understand me." He grabbed Jack's face with both hands.

"Put it under his name. That way, it doesn't come back to us, but we get a good chunk of the action." Looking over at Vinny, Giancarlo continued, "And you, Vin, I want you and Jimmy to be the muscle. Make sure Tommy Boy or anyone else don't get outta line, sorta keep an eye on the place."

Jimmy Barone was one of Giancarlo's silent but tough soldiers. He was a good earner on the streets, with a reputation as a gentle giant to those who didn't know what he did for a living. *Giant Jim,* the hefty six-foot-six, 450-pound soldier, was very loyal to Giancarlo and never questioned any *of the Cat's* requests. He was also an enforcer. The boss depended on him for the muscles but not so much for the brains.

The very next day, the Broad Street Gentlemen's Club in Newark was under new management. The lease had been under Eddy's name, but the landlords had no problem dissolving the old one and putting a new lease under Tommy Boy's name. Giancarlo was not as *big of a fish* as many of the other mob bosses in New York or New Jersey were. However, he was a wealthy, respected businessman who had many connections.

As the days passed, the club was bringing in large amounts of cash again. Most of the same girls whom Rose had recruited had stayed. Yet Rose had no idea what was transpiring. She spent most of her days out of the house, in Manhattan, avoiding everyone.

Rose loved Manhattan. Aside from the obvious tourist sites such as Times Square or the Empire State Building, she loved its fascinating neighborhoods, trendy boutiques, and charming cafés and bars.

Lately Manny would accompany her often. Still, he liked to take care of his own matters now and again, and she would go alone. Unfortunately, Rose had no idea what his "own matters" were other than hang around Brooklyn Heights and meet up with friends.

How Rose wished he would be more like his father and get into the family business. Manny occasionally stopped by the factory and offices. However, her hopes were that Manny would completely take over, and then she could become the *top* socialite of their social circle.

In Rose's view, Giorgia was too old and washed up to be the leading lady any longer. Mara? Well, Mara was much too immature and wild to be taken seriously. Who better than she could be more fitting for the role?

At this point, Rose's biggest concerns were far greater than becoming top socialite. What if Giancarlo or Manny found out about her connection to the club? All the strolls in Manhattan could not take her away from her conscience. She would become anxious and fearful every time she had any thoughts of her entanglement. Now that Ricky and Eddy were dead, there were no others who knew about her involvement. But why were they killed in the first place?

As time passed, Giancarlo Catalano and his crew began experiencing a new level of respect from the major mob families. Rumours began to circulate in New York and New Jersey that the Cat and his crew had evolved to higher ground. They were responsible for having two of their own soldiers clipped for betraying the family. In the past, Giancarlo was considered a small player in a big game. He was revered as a serious and vigorous businessman and capo. Respect and loyalty were two of the most important templates among gangsters. Giancarlo, punishing his own soldiers for disobeying these principles, proved his honour to the *code*.

When Rose entered the house after another day in Manhattan, Giorgia called her over into the kitchen.

"Rosie! Rosie, dear, come in here, please." Rose was startled. Since she had arrived, she never had any conversations with her mother-in-law other than during dinners along with everyone else. After walking into the kitchen, Rose noticed Gigi was alone. Not even Gabrielle was anywhere to be seen. This made Rose apprehensive yet delighted at the same time.

"Rosie, dear, Giani and I wanted to wait a little bit—you know, for Mara and the whole Ricky thing to pass. But we really wanna throw a big bash for you and Manny."

"Oh yes, of course, Mrs. Catalano, that would be lovely." Rose beamed.

"Oh, honey, please call me *Ma*. After all, we're family now," assured Gigi. Rose was elated. For the first time since she had arrived, she felt accepted.

Just when Rose thought she was close to being exposed, Giorgia put her at ease. If they had any suspicion of her, they wouldn't be planning to throw a party, she reassured herself.

"I think I should come with you one of these days when you go into the city. We can start looking at some venues and start some plannin'. Giani, Rosie and I are going to go into the city one of these days to book a venue," stated Gigi to Giancarlo when he passed the kitchen. He paused and stared at the two of them for a few seconds. Rose began to tremble. She didn't like the way he was glaring. When she began to feel another panic attack coming on, he simply said, "Sure, good idea. We need to move on now, and what better way than to throw a nice, big shindig?" Rose was relieved. Finally, her life in America was starting to progress.

Rose and Manny's relationship had started to mend. Her in-laws were finally accepting her. Ricky and Eddy were permanently out of the picture. Now she was going to have the big wedding soiree of her dreams. She could relax and reap the benefits of being a wealthy American bride and socially prominent woman. Little did she realize the general society looked upon the Catalanos as only a sleazy, vulgar mob *famiglia*. Any respect Giancarlo did receive from the *outsiders* was only due to his productive fashion career.

Rose was fully aware of her new family's other business interests and dealings. Still, unlike the gangsters of Naples, American mobsters were admired and glorified, especially during this era. The rise of Las Vegas and California as gangster hot spots was making many gangsters famous. She didn't look at American gangsters as violent, ruthless hoodlums like the Italians. The Italian American mobster was wealthy, successful, and powerful. They were deemed more *heroic* than the Neapolitan criminals she was accustomed to back in Italy.

Mara was still grieving the death of her fiancé. Yet her grieving process was not the usual crying and dark period most people went through from the death of a loved one. Her mourning period consisted of heavy drinking and lots of partying. Although she had spurts, it was this lack of sorrow that persuaded Gigi to move forward with preparations for her son's grand gala.

Rose was more than happy to oblige. They barely waited after their kitchen meeting took place to begin. The very next day, Gigi and Rose were off to the city to look at venues and start the planning. Although they lived in Brooklyn Heights, Gigi insisted the reception be held in Manhattan. The venues in Brooklyn were just not extravagant enough to host the kind of party that would make a statement. She only wanted Rose and Manny to have their religious ceremony in a Catholic church in Brooklyn.

Rose anticipated seeing many venues with her mother-in-law; however, it seemed Gigi already had one in mind. When Rose walked into Cipriani's Forty-Second Street, she herself didn't mind. Cipriani's was magnificent. Mirroring the Italian Renaissance, it was just what Rose had envisioned for her wedding one day. Colossal arches, marble and mosaics, enormously high ceilings—it was an absolute dream. After spending a few hours examining the setting and coordinating the menu with the top chef, the ladies couldn't wait to head home to further discuss their plans with Giancarlo and Manny.

That night, when Giancarlo heard of a church ceremony during dinner, he quickly discouraged the idea.

"What the fuck they need the church for? You know Father Ignatius don't like us, plus they already got married in Italy. We're just gonna have a reception." Manny kept his head down and continued eating while Gigi looked dubiously over to Rose.

Why was he so adamant about them not having a religious ceremony? Rose was speechless and furious her husband didn't utter a word. Then Rose contemplated, *What purpose would a church ceremony serve anyway?* She and Manny were already married in a civil ceremony back in Portici.

As long as they were legally married, nothing else mattered to Rose now. All she really wanted was a grand reception anyway—a lavish gathering of all the Catalanos' social circle. This would be her debut into the opulent world of one of New York's finest fashion families.

Even if the Catalanos were not considered big-time players when it came to the underworld, having a successful garment industry was what made them prominent. Since the deaths of Ricky and Eddy, the crew had begun to gain more clout. Even Rose noticed the uprising of their authority quite quickly.

From the word on the street to the increase of activities surrounding the family, Giancarlo's reputation and influence had gained tremendous praise and respect. Even his crew began gaining more notoriety. After dinner, Giancarlo went to sit in his studio to have a glass of his signature cognac drink when Jack and Sammy entered.

"Cat, man, we got some great news," Sammy blurted.

"Oh yeah, what's that?" Giancarlo grinned. He had a good inkling as to what they were referring to. He thought he would have them tell him first before he got his hopes up high.

"Frank and Vito are all for that meetin'. It's finally lookin' good for us, Cat," ranted Jack.

"Well, set it up then. What are you waitin' for?" urged Giancarlo.

"Mr. C, something just arrived for you," Gabrielle announced after walking into the studio.

"What it is, Gabby?"

"It's from Italy. Looks like a paintin' of some kind," noted Gabrielle.

"Great, have it brought up here," directed Giancarlo.

"A paintin', huh? What kind of paintin'?" inquired Jack.

"It's a gift I want to present to my son and his bride. But it's no one's business until the reception," joked Giancarlo.

"I can't believe all the shit you're doin' after what that *puttana* did to us behind our backs with those two fucks," Sammy asserted.

"Take it easy. Don't worry about it right now. I'm gonna handle it my way," Giancarlo reassured.

When the courier gentleman brought in the painting, Sammy and Jack left. Giancarlo paused after hearing shouting coming from the lower level. It was Mara screaming at her mother.

"That bitch gets a reception at Cipriani's, and mine was going to just be at the Grand Prospect? What the fuck?"

"Just? Just at Grand Prospect? That's a gorgeous place, you ungrateful little shit!" Gigi yelled back. "Now get your drunk ass up in your bed, and sleep that shit off! Gabrielle! Take this ingrate upstairs!" Then Gigi, looking over at Mara, continued, "And I don't want to see your wretched face until you sober up! You got me?"

As Gabrielle walked Mara up to her room, Giancarlo could hear his daughter wailing. He purposely didn't look at them as they passed the studio. He sat in his chair with his back to the door. Although what he had done with Ricky was what was needed, it broke his heart to see his daughter's despair. Even Giancarlo himself never would have believed he would go to those extremes. Then he reminded himself, *Sometimes you just gotta do whatcha gotta do.*

The grand reception validating her marriage to her gorgeous American GI was three weeks away, and Rose had never been more elated. Manny noticed his wife's euphoria but still couldn't get Lili out of his mind. He had hoped all this excitement would elate him too, but the thought of Lili made him somber and bitter. She was thousands of miles away beyond the sea, in another sphere. Would he ever see her again? he speculated.

"Gig! I gotta go," advised Giancarlo to his wife.

"Where you goin' now?" demanded Gigi. Giancarlo never answered to his wife. She sat down at the kitchen table and began crying. Manny came down.

"Ma, you okay? What's goin' on? I heard talkin' and shit." Manny consoled his mother with a rub on her back as he sat down beside her. Manny knew his mother was eccentric, but she hardly ever cried. This was unusual for her.

"Manny, you know I never questioned your father."

"Yeah, Ma, I know. Why, what's up?" he asked with concern.

"I think your father is having an affair," Giorgia stated.

"Affair? What the fuck you talkin' about? He's too busy with his business to even give it to you, let alone another broad," joked Manny thinking he would get a laugh. "Ma, come on. Where's all this bullshit comin' from, huh?"

"You know your father goes to the factory during the day, but in the evenings, he conducts his business here, in the studio. Lately, he's goin' out a lot at night when the factory is closed! Where the fuck's he goin'?" snapped Gigi.

"Ma! Take it easy. I'll look into it, okay? Don't worry about it."

Manny had also noticed his father's absence lately. Where was he going? His mother was right. During the day, Giancarlo liked to pass by the factory to make sure everything was running smooth, maybe meet friends for coffee or lunch at Mammy's Pantry once in awhile. But he always came home for dinner and did any business dealings in his studio. Giancarlo was also a man of routine, and this was way off his habitual schedule.

At his mother's request, Manny decided to follow his father one night. He borrowed his friend Benny Barbieri's mint-green Chevrolet Fleetline. Giancarlo would never recognize the car since he didn't even really know Benny. Manny waited for him down the street one night.

Where the hell is he going? wondered Manny. This was farther than where Giancarlo would normally go. As his father drove out of Brooklyn and onto the Marine Parkway Bridge, Manny was beginning to feel really uneasy. Why would his father be heading toward Long Beach? *If he's having an affair, how did he even meet a broad from there?* Manny speculated. Giancarlo usually hung around the neighborhood and periodically went into Manhattan. But Long Beach?

Manny managed to stay close enough to Giancarlo's car so as not to lose him but far enough that his father wouldn't suspect anything. Giancarlo drove into the driveway of a beautiful Georgian mansion along Shore Road. It was a grand estate that stuck out from the other more traditional Cape Cod–style bungalows. Whoever lived here was definitely wealthy, thought Manny. It was a white two-story home designed with pillars and columns around a templelike entrance, with a portico, fitted with a pediment over the large mahogany-wood door. Giancarlo walked up and rang the doorbell.

While Manny waited impatiently for the door to open, he kept reciting to himself, "Please don't let it be a woman." As soon as it did, Manny's heart felt like it had dropped into his stomach. It was a woman. His mother was right. Giancarlo was probably having an affair. After kissing the woman on the cheek, he walked inside.

Who the hell is that? he speculated. He didn't see much of her, but he did notice she was a voluptuous, buxom, yet petite woman, not overweight but definitely not thin. Wearing a light-colored fitting dress, she reminded him of an older version of Lili, only this woman had dark hair. Manny finally drove away. He didn't want to wait outside the house. He wasn't sure how long his father would be, and he had seen enough for the night.

CHAPTER TWELVE

The day had arrived. Lilianna and her son, Gian-Paolo, had finally reached the United States of America. As soon as the MS *Volcania* entered the New York harbor, Lili and her son were some of the first people to disembark. The anticipation was so intense, she didn't even sleep in her room the last night. Lili made sure she had front row so she could get off the vessel as soon as possible.

After walking off the ship, Lili couldn't see anyone fitting the description that the dottore had given her. Then she realized he hadn't given much of a summary of this woman who was coming for her. All Lili knew was her name was Letizia. She and her son were quickly guided to the customs area. There they were first checked for trachoma, a highly contagious eye disease, and medically examined. Then they had to pass through immigration inspection. Once that was completed, Lili would be directed to the ground floor to wait for a ferry to transport them to Manhattan.

Lili became confused and overwhelmed.

What do I do now? she fretted. Was this woman Letizia standing by closely? Or was she going to be waiting in Manhattan once she got off the ferry? As she was standing still and not knowing what to do, one of the immigration officers demanded she get on the ferry. Now she knew she had no choice but to go.

With her son in her arms, Lili wept the whole time on the ferry ride. She was petrified and shaken. Where was she going? At least in Italy, she knew her way around, but this was New York, a place she had only heard about and seen pictures of, a strange, exciting land many only got to dream about. But here she was, actually there.

What am I going to do? Lili panicked.

When she finally arrived, Lili hadn't even got off the ferry when she noticed a distinctive-looking woman standing next to a silver Rolls Royce Phantom III limousine.

"There she is," Lili whispered to herself. She didn't know how, but she knew this was her. This was Letizia, an attractive, sophisticated petite woman. She was dressed in an elegant dark suit and wore a large-brimmed hat and gloves. Holding a cigarette in her hand, she immediately turned to her chauffer, who then approached Lili.

Oddly, Letizia also noticed Lili right away. The fact that Lili had a child in her arms might have given it away, but there were several young girls with children. Yet there was just something about Lilianna that Letizia had a hunch about. The two of them identified each other immediately, like no one else was around.

"Signora Fabbri?" guessed Lili after approaching her. Letizia smiled and placed her hand on Lili's cheek.

"Yes, my sweet. Please. You must be tired." She directed her to get into the car. "When we get to the house, Valentina will be there to take care of anything you need."

"You are very kind, signora. Grazie," Lili mumbled nervously.

"No need to thank me now, dear. But soon you will." Letizia winked.

When they reached Letizia's home, Lili gazed in quiet amazement. Everything looked so beautiful, so green, not gray like what she had been used to back in Italy. When she walked out of the car, Lili took the deepest breath she had ever taken and exhaled in relief. She didn't know how long she would be living in *this* house but knew this was her home.

Lili realized Rose was also in New York, probably not far from her. That meant Manny was too. What would Rose do if she ever saw her and her son? What would Manny do? So many thoughts were consuming her mind while she was unpacking.

Lili only had a few items to put away in her new sleeping quarters. However, anything and everything else she would need was already there in the room. It was spacious and bright, with a king-size bed and a beautiful, ornate antique oak Victorian bassinet next to it for her baby.

Only thirty miles away, Rose, along with her new mother-in-law, was busy planning the most exciting night of her life. She couldn't wait any longer even though it was only a few days away. The week leading up to the celebratory evening was just as exciting. With gifts arriving and last-minute details being confirmed, Rose couldn't wait to get into her new white satin gown. It had a sweetheart neckline and an A-line skirt. Since she wore a hat for the civil ceremony, she felt it fitting to wear a tiara for the reception.

Rose and Giorgia wanted Manny to wear his uniform. Although it reminded him too much of his time in Italy and especially of Lili, he agreed. Giancarlo was also anticipating the night. It had been a long time since he and his wife hosted a grand reception. He knew this was going to be a night many of them would never forget, especially the bride and groom.

The evening had finally arrived. Even Cipriani's hadn't looked that beautiful in a long time, especially since the war had begun. People didn't have the cash flow as they did before, so many were rationalizing and not spending as much—except the Catalanos. They had an abundance of money and weren't afraid to show or spend it, more so when it came to their children. They couldn't give Mara the glamorous wedding she wanted, so they decided to provide for Manny.

Manny wasn't much into glitzy, extravagant affairs, but this was the wish of his parents and his new bride. Knowing he wasn't attentive and considerate to Rose during their first few weeks together, this was his way of showing her that he would change and accept their union.

That night, Rose felt like a real princess. She was ecstatic and delirious. She and Manny began to greet the three hundred guests as they entered the magnificent ballroom. It was a breathtaking venue already, but with the added candelabras and flowers, it was truly magical. Rose knew she would be the center of attention; after all, she was the beautiful bride. All eyes were on her, just the way she liked it. Finally, she was being introduced into the Catalano domain. Manny pondered, if only all this exuberance was for him and Lili, not him and Rose.

There was plenty of Dom Perignon brut champagne, and guests dined on spinach and cheese ravioli with asparagus, filet mignon with a peppercorn sauce, mixed salad, and assorted Italian cheeses. After the dinner, Giancarlo asked Jack and Sammy to meet him outside for a cigarette before he was to make his speech and present the couple with his gift.

"Sam, did you get ahold of our friends over in Naples?" Giancarlo inquired.

"Yeah, Cat, everything is set. The Nucci brothers will be waitin', and we don't gotta worry no more," reassured Sammy.

"Good. I want it taken care of as soon as possible," Giancarlo demanded.

"Sure thing, Cat. Don't worry about it. Just go in there and have some fun tonight." Jack chuckled.

"Oh, you better believe this is going to be fun," asserted Giancarlo sarcastically

It was time for the father of the groom to get up and give a toast and blessings to his son and his son's *wife*. Although he loathed this woman, especially since she betrayed him, he gave a short but simple speech. Then it was time for him to present Rose and Manny with his special gift.

"Thanks to all of you, my family and friends, for joining us on this unforgettable evening. But before I conclude, I wanted to present my son and his lovely bride an exquisite gift I purchased while I was in the motherland, bella Italia."

Giancarlo raised his glass and winked.

"Salute!" Two of the banquet servers placed the painting in front of Rose and Manny. After it was unveiled, the guests gasped in wonder while Manny and Rose were perplexed and baffled—that was until Giancarlo began to explain the incredible yet mysterious canvas.

"I present to both of you this beautiful work of art." Giancarlo stared at Rose with a bitter, demonic glare. He continued, "It's a masterpiece by Dante Gabriel Rossetti from 1868. He called it *Lady Lilith*. Isn't it beautiful, folks? Do you believe she was considered a demon and evil temptress? I think she looks more like a sweet angel to me, kinda like your baby sister, huh, Rose." Giancarlo chuckled. He continued, "It's a shame Lilianna and husband, Luca, couldn't join us. I had the pleasure of meeting both of them when I was in Italy recently and their beautiful baby boy."

Husband, Luca? Baby boy?

Manny and Rose could not disguise their horrified faces. The guests were left bewildered. The mural was beautiful, but why did the bride and groom look so troubled instead of grateful?

"Is this a joke?" Manny blurted.

"Isn't she beautiful, son?" jested Giancarlo as he pointed to the painting.

"What's going on?" inquired Gigi, noticing the strange reaction from her son and his bride.

As a drunken Mara took to the microphone to give her best wishes, her quick disruption managed to shift the attention from *Lady Lilith*. Rose couldn't contain her disbelief and emotions. How could such a magical evening turn into such a nightmare? It was at that moment, she realized her father-in-law was retaliating. He definitely knew about her liaison with his soldiers and the gentlemen's club. The shock was so intense she almost collapsed and had to hold herself up.

Rose excused herself, claiming she didn't feel well, and went to the ladies' room. The guests began to dance. It was announced the dance floor was open as the big band began to play. Manny was in a rage. When the father and son stormed outside, Jack and Sammy followed.

"What the fuck was that shit all about?" Manny screamed. "In front of all these people, you humiliate us?"

Giancarlo looked over at his consigliere and underboss and affirmed, "Remember when I said I wanted that matter taken care of as soon as possible? Well, I want it done tonight! It's time."

"Sure thing, Cat," Sammy reassured.

"Listen, Manny! Calm the fuck down!" insisted Giancarlo.

"Calm down? Are you fucking kidding me? What the fuck is wrong with you?" screamed a visibly shaken Manny.

"In time, you'll thank me, but now I gotta go. Jackie, make sure Gabrielle took care of all the other shit," Giancarlo stressed as he got into a vehicle and drove away.

"Where the fuck you goin'? What the fuck is happenin'?" Manny pleaded with Jack and Sam. "Gabrielle? What the fuck does she have to do with anythin'? What shit?"

"Manny, listen." Jack put his arm around him. "I know this is lousy timing and you're a little fucked up about it, but trust me. Your father had to do what he had to do."

"But she's my fucking wife!" asserted Manny.

"Your wife is a fuckin' *puttana*! Just like her mother. She was shacking up with Ricky, and the two of them, along with that bobo, Eddie, were running a whorehouse in Newark," Jack explained. "The three of them were going behind all our backs and hidin' cash."

"No fucking way!" snapped Manny.

"Yup! Gabby got all her stuff out, and she's going back to Naples, where she belongs!" Sammy spit.

"What the fuck are you sayin'?" Manny put his head in his hands. "That son of a bitch! He thinks *my* wife is a whore? Where the fuck did he go now, huh? To his fucking whore?" As Manny got into a car, Jack and Sammy tried restraining him. But he managed to get in and drive away.

When Manny sped off, Giorgia came out screaming, "What the hell is going on? Where's Manny going? And where's Rose?"

"Gigi, just go back inside, and if people ask anything, just tell them the bride and groom wanted to start their honeymoon early tonight. Now, go finish the night. Everything will be explained when you get home. For now, don't ask any questions," Jack asserted.

Sammy guided Gigi back into the ballroom then Vinny and Jimmy arrived. They were there to quietly take Rose to the port. This would be the last time anyone would ever see her again. With a gun poking at her side, they escorted her into a car. She did not cause any scene or make any noise. Her night of triumph and jubilance turned into a night of disaster and terror.

Manny knew exactly where his father was going. He had followed Giancarlo before to a Long Beach house, which he was convinced was the home of his father's *mistress*. After a harrowing drive, which surprisingly didn't end in an accident, Manny arrived at the house. When he reached the front entrance, he started pounding with both fists. The housemaid quickly answered, and before she could even say anything, Manny stormed inside. He found Giancarlo with a woman sitting in the salon.

"What the fuck did you do to my wife?" demanded Manny.

"She ain't your wife, never was," Giancarlo confirmed. "No record of the two of you ever gettin' married," he added. "Let her go. She's a lyin' whore who was fucking your sister's fiancé and running a whorehouse!"

Giancarlo had made an offer to the mayor of Portici while in Italy. He reminded him of the ruins his town was in and that they could use lots of cash. So the American businessman agreed to "donate" money to help rebuild it. In exchange, the municipality of Portici would dissolve the marriage certificate of Manuele Catalano to the local girl Rosanna Bianchi. The mayor agreed without hesitation.

Manny's night of bliss and acceptance turned into a night of madness and turmoil.

"You're with this bitch, but my wife's a whore?" raged Manny.

"I'm sorry? Bitch?" retorted the woman.

"Ohhhhh! Zio Francesco, this is his wife, Letti," Giancarlo clarified.

"You're fuckin' your dead friend's fuckin' wife?" scolded Manny.

"I ain't fuckin' Frankie's wife! She's been helping' me!" Giancarlo snapped.

"Actually, we've been helping you, Manuele," informed Letizia.

Manny looked at her, baffled.

"Come." Letizia directed them to the end of the staircase. "Valentina, please go and get our guests."

"Si, si, signora."

"Oh my god! What the fuck is goin' on tonight?" Manny agonized with his head in his hands. When he looked back up, there she was. It was Liliana, the real love of his life. Manny was stunned. How could this be? How did she get here?

Her coming down the stairs was like an illusion. Manny was so entranced; he couldn't move.

"Manuele." Lili began to weep as they both embraced each other tightly. Manny couldn't control his elation. Cupping her face in his hands, he gulped.

"I can't believe it is you!"

Before bringing Rose to the pier, Vinny and Jimmy, along with Jack and Sammy, made one more stop along the way. The Crazy Cat wanted his daughter-in-law to say goodbye to her baby sister one last time.

After they all entered the home, Rose became crippled. There in her lavish wedding gown, she stood before her adversary, *Lilith*, who was with her husband, Manny.

"Before you go, I thought it would be only *fair* you say goodbye to your baby sis—oh, and your new nephew."

Rose stared at Gian-Paolo and couldn't deny the resemblance to Manny. She of all people knew that even if Lili had been married to Luca, this child couldn't possibly be his.

For the first time ever, Rose witnessed her wholesome Lili and honorable Manny become heartless and insensitive just like she had always been. Neither one of them seemed affected. Neither of them said or did anything to prevent her upcoming fate. Rose knew this was the end for her in America. They were sending her back to

Naples, where she would be met by the Nucci brothers, who were members of the Di Lauro Camorra *famiglia*. Once there, she would be placed in a brothel to work as a prostitute, entered into the same trade as her mother was entangled in.

After Rose was taken away, Manny turned to Lili.

"You have a son?"

"*Our* son," confirmed Lili.

Manny began sobbing uncontrollably. "I love you, *Lady Lilith*."

She began to giggle. Valentina then handed Gian-Paolo to him. With his arms around his *lady* and his son, Manny looked over at his father and mouthed the words, "Thank you."

ABOUT THE AUTHOR

Carm Ianiri is a Canada-based writer who has had a successful career as an administrative coordinator and assistant in the education sector for many years. Residing in Whitby, Ontario, Carm has been working for the district school board and in colleges for over a decade while fulfilling her dream of becoming an author.

Carm began her college career as an instructor, paving the way to additional avenues in education, including student-placement coordinator and admissions officer. From assisting and advising students of all ages in fulfilling their future goals, Carm gained the grit to aspire to her own ambitions. While Carm was encouraging and guiding her students to ensure their success, they, in turn, inspired her in executing her objectives.

As she was raised in the Italian culture, one of Carm's favorite pastimes, aside from eating, is gathering with family and relatives. Listening to the elderly recount many memories from the past has bolstered her admiration of stories from preceding eras, especially during World War II. Carm spent endless hours and days with her now-deceased grandmother, who narrated countless war stories of hardships, love, lies, betrayal, and death.

Carm's hunger for exhilarating and risqué narratives are a spicy paradox to her love of animals, family, and food. She is married and is a mama to her dog, cat, and lovebird. Carm appreciates the simple life yet still revels in adventure and bustle. Her passion and interest in sensual, impudent stories has inspired her to make up her own brazen tales reflecting characters and accounts of former folks.